# Longhand and Lotsmore

Adam Scribentis

Published by Adam Scribentis, 2024.

## Copyright and credits

---

1.  http://dreamstime.com
2.  http://socreativestudio.us

# Table of Contents

# For the Reader's Most Kind Attention

*Longhand and Lotsmore* is the final form of a tale conceived in 1999, completed and revised in 2011/12, left fallow for a decade and revised again for publication from 2022 to 2024. Almost all of its narrative elements were in place by 2011/12. In the last phase of revision, some modifications to the plot were made for reasons of narrative logic, not for the sake of topicality. The storyteller thanks all who, for friendship or money (or both), have aided and abetted the progress of the work.

The story is set, for the most part, in the Republic of Sardoniki, an imaginary Greek-speaking country of Eastern Europe. The characters and events are fictional. What is more, any similarity of name between any of the characters and any real person of the present or recent past is (it ought to go without saying) entirely coincidental. The same applies to the fictional institutions and companies in the story. The names of imaginary cities and countries have been invented or are used fictitiously. And neither the General's Kokoni nor Mr Ben Ezra's tabby is based on *your* dog or cat.

# How to pronounce the Greek names in this story

Many of the Greek names that occur here really exist as names, some are genuine Greek nouns or adjectives co-opted as names, others have been invented. Several names are archaic in form: the Republic of Sardoniki is not Greece, and its dialect includes forms that are not current in Demotic Greek.

The mythological names *Cassandra, Cerberus, Cyclops, Hercules, Prometheus* and *Semele* are given in their Latin forms, and their usual English pronunciation is supposed. All other Greek names, including forms of Semitic names, are transcribed to reflect modern Greek pronunciation. These are listed below, with each name marked for stress. Additional points of pronunciation are noted at need. The names are grouped in order of occurrence, after the number of the chapter and episode in which they occur for the first time.

I.1. Nía, Kallístos Leonídis, Athanasía, Kosmás, Stéfas, Daríos, Línos, Spýros, Rávdos, Kratistópolis, Sardoníki, Sevastós, Dalmátios, Koprónymos, Apollonía, Vasílissa Athemístou.

Note: *e* is pronounced as in English *red*, *i* and *y* like *ee* as in *see*. *d* is pronounced like *th* in *father*. *Dalmatios* has four syllables (*Dal-má-ti-os*).

I.2. Kónon Konstantínou, Léaina, Lígdos.

Note: *ai* also sounds like *e* as in *red*. *Leaina* has three syllables (*Lé-e-na*).

I.3. Erithía, Theodoúlos, Éftropos, Papías, Sympósion, Vássos Várvaros.

I.4. *Dikaiópolis.*

II.1. Láios Aígagros, Ópsiva, Lázaros, Aspasía.

Note: The *ai* of *Laios* is pronounced *ey* as in *whey* (*Léy-os É-ga-gros*).

# Peter Lotsmore's Song

*To a tune by Holst*

Duty called and sent me serving in a land across the sea,

Where a strange, hard queen sat waiting, with soldier's work for me.

Queen of arms and occult payment, credit failed the words she said,

And there lay, for all her lying, the wounded and the dead.

The archangel's note rings cryptic at the running of her guns:

I fly back to you, Vasilissa, the route doom also runs!

# I. MONDAY

# I.1. The Invigilator

The General was standing with his back to Nia as she picked up a fallen weapon and charged towards him amid the debris of combat. Taking expert aim at him, she squeezed the trigger, shouting at the top of her voice: "I am the Queen of the guerrillas, *and you're dead!*"

In the mirror by the wardrobe, where he was straightening his tie, General Kallistos Leonidis saw Nia's mother take hold of her and swing her out of the way. "Leave Daddy alone now, dear," said Athanasia. "He has to see the President this morning."

"Yerk!" said Nia's older brother, Kosmas. "The Wicked Witch!"

"Where did you hear that?" Athanasia snapped back at him.

"That's what Uncle Stefas said," replied the seven-year-old.

"Well, we don't repeat everything Uncle Stefas says," Athanasia retorted, with more vehemence than conviction.

The General turned and made towards the door. His wife intercepted him. "I don't suppose you'll find out today when you can take your leave?"

"No," he said. "I'm sure that's not on the agenda."

Athanasia persisted. "Will you be here for Darios's birthday?"

"We'll see."

"You know – " Athanasia was interrupted by a whine of distress, followed by a chuckle of anarchic malice, rising from the room off to the left.

"Darios!" she shouted. "Stop torturing Linos: he doesn't appreciate it." She turned back to her husband. "You know it's Darios's birthday on Thursday."

The General nodded. "I know."

"Have you ever been here for his birthday?"

"I'm sure I have," he replied. "At least once."

"When?"

"Oh, about five years ago."

"Darios is four!" the protest began. It was broken off when Athanasia noticed the grin that told her that her husband's watch, which he was now consulting, was not the only thing he had been winding up.

"Look, I have to be going," he apologized. "Mustn't keep the Witch waiting."

Athanasia shook her head.

"Are you going to give her hell?" Kosmas asked gravely.

"No, son," said the General, laying his hand on the boy's head. "I'm afraid," he sighed, "it's going to be entirely the other way round." He kissed Athanasia's cheek placatingly (or so he hoped), rubbed the ears of Spyros, the benignly watchful Kokoni, and returned the wave of six-year-old Nia, who, having blithely blown him off the battlefield, apparently did not mean him to take it personally. Leaving the house, he was met by his aide, Major Ravdos, who was waiting for him with the staff car that would drive them to the Cabinet Office in Kratistopolis, the capital of Sardoniki.

The Republic of Sardoniki, governed by an elected ruling president from the majority party of the legislature, borders on Ghimir to the south and Krastina to the south-east. It is ninety-six per cent Greek-speaking (with its own dialect) and ninety-five per cent Orthodox; the air is warm but respirable; its politics are volatile but usually of no more than marginal interest to the outside world. At that moment, however, the designs of the Western Intergovernmental Arms and Security Convention (WIASCO) had given the country a strategic significance that drew it out of its obscurity. Hostilities between the border tribes of the Rustim and the Haman were apt to provide a *casus belli* against President Kalgan of Ghimir, neighbour and supporter of the Haman. The two tribes were the remainder of the peoples whose incursion into Sardoniki in the thirteenth century had been halted by the national hero King Sevastos, who was yet never able to dislodge them entirely. Hence the Disputed Zone; hence, too, the session of the President's Council on Internal and External Security to which the General was now travelling.

It was the feast day of Sardoniki's patron saint, the tenth-century bishop and martyr Dalmatios. Kopronymos, the Governor of Sardoniki, had employed a heathen bodyguard from the North, led by Bodvar Seal-biter. The Bishop had always been opposed to this policy, having had experience of Norse adventurers from his time in the Emperor's service. At that time there was a noble lady in the province, Mother Apollonia, who lived as a recluse. One day, one of Bodvar's boys approached her and attempted gallantry, whereupon the venerable lady drew the man's sword from its scabbard and killed him on the spot. His kinsmen did what was expected of them and burned the hermitage with its occupant. Bishop Dalmatios demanded action of the Governor, and when the Governor failed to give satisfaction, he excommunicated him. Soon afterwards, the Bishop was ambushed by Norsemen, who trapped him, with his retinue, in a ring of fire. The saint walked through the fire and came out unharmed on the other side, only to be felled by the bowmen of the ambushing party. The Patriarch of Constantinople vindicated the martyred Bishop, so that the Governor was required to expel Bodvar and his men as a condition for having the excommunication lifted. Kopronymos, who had not entirely escaped public suspicion in the matter, had little choice but to comply. The Norsemen made a last attempt to hold on to one corner of land, but all fell when it came to a fight. The saint is said to have prophesied this to his companions in the ring of fire, and, before he walked out to his death, to have encouraged them with a final enigma: "He who sleeps, let him wake up!"

The feast of Saint Dalmatios is not an official public holiday. Nevertheless, half the capital was more or less taking the day off to decorate the streets with palms and flags. It would, of course, require a further day off on Tuesday to take them down. In short, Kratistopolis was enjoying a particularly long weekend. People loafed about the streets; cheery, stocky lads and big, laughing girls chattered and flirted in the mellow September sun. The General smiled briefly as he passed them by, his car holding its sober course for the Cabinet Office.

"Do you know what they want with us this time?" the General asked casually.

"No idea, sir," replied the Major, duplicating the impression of nonchalance, "except that some official from the Convention is sitting in."

In the conference room, they found the other members of the Security Council already assembled. The Vice-President sat on the left; in the next places sat the Defence Secretary and the Secretary of State for the Interior. The Foreign Secretary and the Attorney General sat opposite them, a little further down the table from a man the General had not seen before. This, he supposed, was the WIASCO official. The short, monochrome figure of the Vice-President appeared all the more slight and tenebrous next to the person who occupied the chief place at the far end of the table.

In the memoirs of the consummate explorer Duggan Castlemaine, the author tells how he once fell into an obscure pit, landing hard on the dark earth and profiting little from the sunlight skimming the shaft above him. He was aware, however, of the bars of a cage inches away from his face, and of the querulous imperial growl of the creature confined within it. He glimpsed the fangs and muzzle of the tigress as she railed perilously at him; he heard the beast's paw beating against the bars as the claws tore at the narrow space between the cage and him. He knew that as long as he did nothing provocative, such as advancing, the danger of the cat remained potential, and he could stay in its presence unscathed. But the creature's power to pounce, to strike, to dislocate and tear was not diminished. It was constraint, not tameness, that prevailed against the anger of the beast, and he knew that if he was to extract himself from his mishap, he must not forget it.

Such, *mutatis mutandis*, was the General's reaction to the President, who looked up from her place at the conference table as he entered the room.

Her Excellency President Vasilissa Athemistou greeted the General and invited him to be seated. He took his place opposite the President, while Major Ravdos sat down beside him. The President then turned to the stylish occupant of the place nearest her left hand, introducing him as Garrison Duello, the WIASCO official. Under the smiling scrutiny of this guest, the President addressed the assembled Council.

"I think everyone at this Council will agree," she said, "that the Disputed Zone remains the prime security concern, not only of this Government, but of the entire region." There was a general nod of grave assent, although all knew that this went without saying. All were aware, moreover, that by "this Government" the President invariably meant herself. When other members of the Government used the expression, it was often impossible to tell whether they used it in the same exclusive, monarchical sense, or included themselves in it, or even purposefully employed it as a corporate expression so as to include no one in particular. It was a conveniently, if confusingly, polyvalent term.

The President continued. "Neither the Rustim Autonomists nor the Haman, with their claim to belong to our neighbour, are going to go away any time soon. I take it that at least the second of those scenarios is unacceptable to our Convention partners." The WIASCO official nodded with quick sympathy. "Of course," said the President, with just a little too much emphasis, "there is a law against simply arming the Rustim militia so that they can deal with the Haman in their own way."

No one in the room was ignorant either of that law or of its occasion. The last time that a government had been caught pursuing policy by the said means, Kalgan of Ghimir had risen up at once with his finger on the trigger. War had been averted only by a swift change of government, the incoming one displaying proof of its virtue by the enactment of equally swift legislation: the present Paragraph 13 of the penal code.

"Another dead end," Vasilissa continued, "would be the creation of a no-man's land between the two tribes. Although our immediate predecessors tried it, the resulting military disaster – " (here she caught the General's eye) " – was the end of that solution."

"An entire mine-clearance team was lost, isn't that right?" said Garrison Duello. "A Haman ambush, if I'm not mistaken."

General Leonidis corrected him. "There were two survivors. One was ours; the other was a British officer assigned to our operations in the Zone."

He had clearly spoken out of turn. "The President has not forgotten," the Vice-President told him tartly. "As a minister at the Defence Department, she interviewed the survivors."

The General glanced at the President, who seemed to be taking no interest in the interruption. He looked back at the Vice-President and nodded. "I remember."

The President went on. "Thanks to our Convention partners, we now have a solution. A revised legal framework for security in the Disputed Zone will be presented to Parliament. Today."

General Leonidis turned to Major Ravdos; each read confirmation in the other's face that the President had now come to the point of the meeting. They directed their attention back to her, expecting to hear an account of the promised legal framework.

"Meanwhile," said the President, "what you are about to see is a confidential illustration of the working of the DZ-1-13 satellite, which the Convention has deployed to monitor aerial activity in the Zone. Mr Duello."

The General raised his hand to catch the President's attention, but although she certainly saw him, she ignored his gesture and allowed the WIASCO official to proceed.

"Thank you, Madam President," said Duello. "We greatly appreciate your cooperation, especially in closing the airspace over the Disputed Zone to civilian aircraft. The Army will, of course, have the necessary clearance codes for use once the DZ-1-13 system is operational, that is, from midnight."

All turned to the screen of the conference room. With the aid of graphics, Garrison Duello explained. The satellite would detect any aircraft entering the Disputed Zone, and would hold its peace only on recognition of an access code transmitted by the aircraft. Failure to transmit a recognized code would prompt the satellite to instruct a computer, housed at the WIASCO base in the neighbouring territory of Krastina, to launch a "Tag" missile. The graphics showed a spy plane which, for all its desperate, evasive minnowing, failed to shake off the kamikaze piranha tearing up behind, alongside and into it, causing the final explosion and the mid-air scattering of debris that filled the screen.

"Within the family, we call it *The Invigilator*," said Duello.

"Since there are no questions," said the President, "we will proceed to the second matter that concerns us here, which is – "

General Leonidis raised his hand again. This time the President could not see him, for she had been looking at her brief and had not raised her eyes from it. The Vice-President peered down the table at the General, but otherwise made no response to his gesture. The Secretary of State for the Interior also looked towards General Leonidis, but then turned away to stare past the shoulder of the Attorney General. In the end, it was Garrison Duello who interrupted the President.

"Madam President, I think General Leonidis has a question."

Vasilissa, who had the disconcerting ability to raise one eyebrow while the other stayed almost perfectly still, stared straight down the table and questioned the General's intervention in precisely that silent manner.

"That was a *confidential* briefing?" the General queried.

In silence, by which the General understood that she knew very well that he had heard her quite correctly, the President continued to face him until he came to the point.

"Then the system's operation won't be disclosed to Parliament?" the General continued, noting with alarm the amused looks exchanged among the Secretaries of State, and the obvious irritation of Vasilissa and her Vice-President.

"*Nothing* will be said to Parliament," the Vice-President insisted. "Except the fact of the legal framework and the airspace closure. This Government," he went on (behind the unresolvable ambiguity of that expression), "is under no obligation to provide further specification of the collaborative measures taken with our Convention partners."

Confused, the General again had recourse to his aide, Major Ravdos. The President had said that Parliament would be notified that day of the new legal framework (whatever it was) for security in the Zone. Why, then, was the operation of the WIASCO satellite system to be excluded from the notification?

The Secretary of State for Defence glanced cautiously at Vasilissa, seeking permission to intervene. At her nod, he proceeded.

"The point which I think the General is overlooking," he said, "is that once Parliament has been notified of the revised legal framework, all security measures to be implemented in collaboration with any WIASCO agency, under Article 5 (c) of the Convention, will be implicit in that framework. That, of course, is the reason why no such collaborative measures will, as a rule, require discrete specification."

"What this appears to mean, sir," said Major Ravdos, "is that Parliament will be notified that it's no longer going to be notified."

"Is that constitutional?"

The Attorney General intervened. "General Leonidis, I can assure you that the legal basis for our proceedings is well established. In fact, we have threefold authority. First, there is Article 5, regulating intergovernmental collaboration to ensure security, including domestic security, among signatories to the Convention. Secondly, as Mr Secretary has quite rightly pointed out, the general notification to Parliament of the revised legal framework is sufficient. I refer, of course, to Article 12.3 (f) (bis) of our own Constitution. Thirdly, we have the framework itself, which is in fact a clarification of the existing position, namely that the Government may invoke Article 5 (c) of the Convention in respect of any security measures, domestic or regional, and on the basis of that right establish norms of cooperation in accordance with Article 11 (a) and (b). Now, the application of those articles to the current security requirements of the Disputed Zone will constitute, in effect, the prevailing legal framework until this Government, in consultation with its Convention partners, determines otherwise."

The Secretaries of the Foreign Office, Defence and Interior were nodding vigorously in support of the Attorney General's points. Vasilissa kept tightly poised to resume the progress of the meeting. Only deference to the Attorney General mitigated her obvious impatience.

"The next matter," she announced, "is security for the public lecture on the Urkundendorf Charter which the Vice-President will give tomorrow morning. The Patriotic League has announced a demonstration, and there are, of course, other forces pressing for a No vote in the referendum that could easily multiply the number of protestors several times."

"Including the Holy Synod of the Sardonikan Orthodox Church?" the WIASCO official queried.

"That's correct, Mr Duello," was all that the President would say on that subject.

"What exactly is their problem?"

Since Vasilissa did not reply immediately, the Secretary of State for the Interior took this as permission to fill the lacuna. "They say that Article 2 compromises the constitutional status of the Orthodox

Church, and that Article 6, on gender equity, is injurious to public morals and impedes the exercise of religion."

The General looked up just enough to notice the round of pained smiles and sniggers, then looked away.

"However," Interior continued, "they have accepted a special negotiator from the Holy See. An English Monsignor from the Diplomatic Service."

Duello was amused. "Will that help?"

"It might," said Interior. "Yes, I know, the Holy See likes *reservations* and *qualifying language* and so on, but they are pragmatists. I mean, they're professionals, you have to give them that."

Vasilissa recalled him to business. "Mr Secretary, has the security plan for tomorrow been agreed between your Department and the Urban Containment Division?"

"Yes," said Interior. "I've just received the definitive plan from the Police Commissioner."

General Leonidis did not like to intervene again, but something did not add up. "Excuse me, Mr Secretary, but how many demonstrators from the Patriotic League are you expecting?"

"Oh, not more than a few hundred, I imagine."

"That's not many, and they're usually well behaved. Why is it such a large security issue?"

Interior seeemed somewhat embarrassed. "We understand, too, that Militprol International is planning a counter-demonstration."

General Leonidis glanced at Major Ravdos and saw that his aide was watching the President carefully. The General continued to press the Secretary for the Interior.

"Are the Militprol people already in the city?"

"So we understand."

"And Militprol has members with criminal records in twelve jurisdictions?"

"I don't think the regrettable facts need to be pointed out, General," Interior replied.

"Then, with respect, Mr Secretary," the General continued, "may I ask exactly why the hell they were allowed into the country in the first place?"

"The freedom-of-movement laws – " Interior began, then broke off in frustration, as if the obviousness of the answer made its exposition embarrassingly superfluous.

"The Army is, of course, at your disposal," said the General, "if that would help keep the event free of disturbance."

The Vice-President erupted. "The General knows very well," he seethed, using the third person even while looking across at the General, "that it was precisely because of the historic unreliability, nay, disloyalty of his predecessors, that this Government spent millions developing the Urban Containment Division. If the General thinks that this Government has made that kind of investment, only to reassign the Army to urban security – let him think again before he comes with his pious ideas to this Council!"

There was a smarting silence. All the Council members were embarrassed by the Vice-President's outburst in front of the WIASCO official, but none of them was going to censure him for it. Instead, the rancorous regard of the whole Council was directed down the table at the General himself.

General Leonidis replied with his most innocent smile (which worked, sometimes, with Athanasia). "Pardon me," he said mildly, "but since our Convention – " (he paused, searching for the correct term) " – our Convention *partners* are ensuring security in the Disputed Zone, and the police are now equipped for civil unrest, one might be forgiven for asking whether the Army is undergoing something of a review?"

The President smiled, with a terrible hint of sour pity, a gift of chocolates steeped in vinegar. "General," she assured him, "have no fear of becoming obsolete. There could be a natural disaster, state funeral or firefighters' strike at any time."

The General said no more. Like the admirable Mr Castlemaine, he considered that the way of safety lay in non-provocation.

(Castlemaine, as his readers know, was in fact unlucky. He did indeed escape from the tiger-pit, down a secret tunnel which led all the way to the fabled Chowdhary-Smart Emerald Mines, but not before the tigress had taken a raw, taster-sized helping out of his upper arm as he crept past.)

# I.2. The Doppelgänger

As Peter Lotsmore sat at the airport waiting for his delayed flight to Kratistopolis, he was undeniably feeling below par.

This was nothing new. Although he had recovered well from his accident, there were still days on which his energies were expended simply on staying alert, against the pressure of the lassitude that seeped into his system. Today, he had risen early and was now labouring under the exquisite world-weariness that comes of prolonged exposure to surreal degrees of artificial lighting and the potent scent of stiffly priced coffee. Although his plane had been due to leave at eight a.m., here he was at eight twenty, sitting at the boarding gate, waiting, with low-to-moderate expectations, for an announcement about his flight.

An announcement came. However, it did not give the information he was hoping for. Rather, it was a call to Passenger McCullboy, travelling on the same flight to Kratistopolis, to report to the boarding gate immediately. Peter thought that if they were now trying to round up stray passengers, boarding was probably not far off; on the other hand, it was not going to be in the next five minutes.

At eight thirty, the call for Mr McCullboy was repeated. "Failure to do so will result in your baggage being unloaded from the aircraft, and we regret that you *will* be denied boarding," the girl intoned, a passionless Cassandra. Peter looked at the clock, aware of the sorry likelihood of further delay.

As he waited, he began to be poked by the thought that the name McCullboy ought to mean something to him. No doubt it did. This, too, was not a new experience. Ever since his accident, there were things which he remembered that he knew, without remembering what it was that he knew about them. Sometimes, however, the missing piece would later fall unexpectedly into the puzzle and he would see the picture. Now a thought was jabbing and nudging his brain, with no missing piece in prospect.

Five minutes later came the final call for Mr McCullboy. No one appeared. Peter reflected that Mr McCullboy, whoever he was, would be going nowhere. Still uneasy at this almost-memory, just out of reach of his recall, Peter tried turning his mind to something else. Reaching into his pocket, he drew out a sheet of paper, one that had many times been read, thumbed and folded. Unfolding it once again, he thumbed and read it one more time.

*Dear Peter,*

*We were wondering why we didn't hear from you in the last few years. Now we know. What a story! I'd never have believed it. You'll always be grateful for my parting gift, I think.*

*Come any time if you want to visit. I mean it: come and stay with us. Leaina still makes those pastries: you know, the ones you say have way too much syrup, but never enough to make you say no to them.*

*Everything is pretty much the same here. Except that I left the Army, too. I have my own security company. Not bad. And our favourite pin-up girl from the Defence Department is now running the country. Can you believe that? Leonidis is her Chief of Staff. You'll see when you get here. You will come, won't you? It is my very sincere hope that you will.*

*Your friend,*

*Konon Konstantinou.*

Peter closed up the letter in his palm and pushed it back into his pocket.

By eight fifty the unimpressed congregation of passengers was at last permitted to board the aircraft. The plane was cleared for take-off at nine o'clock, exactly an hour behind schedule. Peter half-paid attention, part courtesy and part curiosity, to the safety features presentation, and no, it had not changed in the five years or more since he had last seen it. As the plane bore hard down the runway and leaped powerfully into the sky, Peter mentally offered a rather formless prayer (he had his rosary on him somewhere, but it was too much effort to hunt for it) and shut his eyes as the cabin lights were dimmed. He dozed, and his memory went ahead of him, back to Sardoniki, to the Disputed Zone.

*The vehicle grinds sulking to a halt and remains stranded among the rocks like a fallen petty dinosaur in the middle of the bare land. Konon Konstantinou is calling their base in the Disputed Zone. A transport will be there within the hour, says Shield Base. Konon disperses the ten-man team around the vehicle in all-round defence. The hour is past.*

*Now it comes. Lead begins tearing into the faces, limbs and trunks of the ring of soldiers. Peter and Konon are still alive; they are closest to the vehicle, and the Haman err by coming out into the open. Using the heavy machine guns, Peter and Konon blast the ground from under the attackers and push them back over the ridge.*

*The wind yawns, and the sky turns a shade dimmer. A signal is coming from inside the transport.*

"Good morning, ladies and gentlemen. My name's Malcolm Landing; I'm Captain on your flight today to Kratistopolis International Airport. I do apologize for the hour's delay in getting us underway this morning. This was due to the impact of an air traffic management decision in relation to our aircraft. That's unfortunate, but we do have to comply. However, we are making good time and we do expect to be arriving in Kratistopolis by one thirty this afternoon, local time."

*Konon Konstantinou screams back at the caller that the team is dead, that he and the British officer are stranded and that the transport should get itself to them immediately. Peter can hear the operator tap dutifully at his keyboard. The sun begins to set, and communications are down.*

*Out of ammunition for the machine guns, Peter and Konon head north-east on foot, leaving the fallen men and vehicle behind. They enter a village, a base of the Rustim militia. There, in their path, stands a spindly adolescent nursing a heavy rifle. He fires on them, and Konon shoots back. A bullet smashes into the guard's forearm. The rifle falls; the boy drops shrieking onto the rough path. A group of militiamen emerge from a house on the right, across the village, steering Peter and Konon away from their building. Villagers appear, angrily attempting to get at the two officers. The militiamen shield them. Behind the wall of armed men, Peter glances around the corner of the building. He sees three vehicles parked there, in various states of health: one scarcely intact, the second grievously pockmarked with rust, the third a sleek, powerful machine with a Kratistopolis number plate.*

*The militiamen grip Peter's shoulders, turn him around, propel him into another building, force him into a seat. Konon, too, is brought in, made to sit. Question after question, fierce and suspicious. Peter loses track of how long this is going on. Konon is handed a telephone and told to call his base. This time a helicopter is with them in thirty minutes.*

*The sequel drags on. Interviews with the top brass. The dead men's families. The press. The enquiry at the Defence Department. The chairs outside the office of the minister, Vasilissa Athemistou. The soft chairs and the cold waiting: Peter and Konon, waiting to see Vasilissa, with nothing more to say between themselves as they sit there. Then the summons into her presence. The cluster of professional award certificates on the wall behind her. The unsmiling young man who transcribes as Vasilissa challenges Konon.*

*"Why didn't you repeat the coordinates when the base called you to confirm them?"*

*"They already had the coordinates."*

*"How can you be sure?"*

*"I gave them the coordinates when I made the first call. I thought they understood that the vehicle hadn't exactly gone anywhere in the meantime."*

*"So you didn't repeat the coordinates?" Vasilissa waits for the answer. A painful pause before the terse reply.*

*"No."*

*The secretary takes down the answer. "Didn't repeat the coordinates," he murmurs as he types.*

*Peter hesitates. Lacking confidence in Sardonikan Greek, he is doubly daunted.* "I think that in the village there was someone from this city who didn't want us to see him."

*Vasilissa turns on him.* "Why do you say that?"

"It would explain the car with the Kratistopolis number plate. And the nervous boy with the gun."

"There is no prohibition on Kratistopolis number plates outside the city, Major Lotsmore."

*I'll give her no sodding prohibition.*

"Are you feeling all right, sir?"

"Sorry?" Peter shifted in his seat. A stewardess with a refreshments trolley was smiling solicitously at him.

"Yes, fine, thank you." It was not true, but it was scarcely a lie. A lifetime of answering *How are you?* with *Fine, thank you* brings the response thoughtlessly to the lips, despite the contradiction of other organs.

"Would you like any refreshments?"

He had better take the opportunity, he thought. It would not be all that long before they arrived, but long enough before lunch.

The plane did indeed make good time, touching down at Kratistopolis just after one twenty-five. Within twenty minutes, Peter was on the transport to the terminal; within thirty minutes, at Passport Control; within thirty-five minutes, at Baggage Reclaim, waiting for his suitcase. Ten minutes later, the conveyor belt began its circuit, sending round and round the inevitable odd item that had not been on the flight, would be claimed by no one, and had been there longer than retrievable memory could ascertain. Fifteen minutes later, a couple of holdalls dropped onto the belt. These, too, went round and round, but none of the encircling passengers moved to take them. Kratistopolis had something in common with many otherwise commodious airports: the purgatorial detention at the baggage belt, with Arrivals just the other side of the sliding doors. Since there was still no sign of his suitcase, Peter took out his cell phone and made a call. Reaching voicemail, he left a message.

"Konon, it's Peter. I suppose you've seen that we've had about an hour's delay. Well, I'm here now, at the airport, just waiting for my suitcase. No idea how much longer it's going to take. You've probably gone for a drink, or something. Anyway, I'll be leaving Baggage Reclaim as soon as I can, then I'll meet you in Arrivals. See you shortly, I hope."

Looking back at the conveyor belt, Peter still had no sight of his suitcase. He walked up and down, eyeing his cell phone, his fingers agitating to make another call. If his luggage had appeared at that moment, the call would not have been made. But the vacant time wheedled him to fill it with the object of his thought. Pushing past a last twinge of hesitation, he selected a United Kingdom number. It couldn't really do any harm, he told himself. Maybe she wouldn't answer, anyway.

"Peter?" There she was.

"Hi, Alice." He heard a disapproving hiss, a sharp edge slicing and cutting him.

"Peter, what are you doing?"

"Just letting you know I've arrived safely. We had a bit of a delay, but we got here all right. Hope you have a good week." He was in trouble, and he knew his rambling would not help.

"You weren't supposed to call me until after you've got back."

"I thought I'd let you know I'm down and safe. I'm here. And I – well – I still care."

Alice sighed. "Yes, Peter, I know you care. But you're not making this any easier. I think we both need this week just to get our thoughts clear. That was the plan. God knows I need it. Have a great time with your friends, and I'll talk to you next week when you get back."

He couldn't bear to end the call while laid so low. He tried one last excuse to keep small-talking. "There's nothing else you've thought of that you want me to bring back?"

"No, Peter. Just bring yourself back after you've had a break. Talk to you later."

"OK. Bye for now."

"Goodbye."

Peter pressed the side button to end the call, wincing and blaming himself for giving in. Now there was nothing to be done but what he ought to have done all along: wait patiently for his suitcase. It came thudding down onto the conveyor belt; he retrieved it, tore off its check-in label and threw the label into the bin. He stepped beyond the doors into Arrivals.

An assortment of placard-holding agents and chauffeurs stood before him. He wove his way through the midst of them, looking left and right, hoping to catch sight of his hosts. He was disappointed. As he stood frowning, considering whether to call Konon again on the cell phone, a sudden voice beside him said: "Mr McCullboy?"

Peter turned to face the speaker, a slight, dark young man, who was addressing him by the name of the passenger who had missed the flight. That was the prompt that Peter's hampered memory had needed, for in that moment, he realized exactly for whom he was being mistaken. It was true that if Drustan McCullboy and Peter Lotsmore were placed side by side, no one would have supposed that they were twins. However, they were of similar height, build and complexion. If someone did not know McCullboy personally, but had, perhaps, been shown a photograph of poor quality, he could easily have made the error, especially if he had been told to expect McCullboy off the plane.

"Mr McCullboy?" the stranger was calling to him.

"Of course!" Peter exclaimed. Since he now recalled who McCullboy was, he spoke aloud to himself, heedless of the ambiguity of his words.

"Delivery tomorrow at five a.m.?" the stranger asked quietly.

Knowing both McCullboy and his line of business, Peter understood what was meant by "a delivery." He also suspected a trap in the question. The trap, if such it was, was for McCullboy, but for the moment he *was* McCullboy, and he feared either to deny the identity or to confirm the request.

"I'm sorry?" he queried.

The stranger was disconcerted. "Just trying to confirm the date and time."

"I'm not sure that we understand each other."

The young man glanced nervously about. "You mean it's not a good moment?"

"You be the judge of that," Peter said wryly.

"I see," the other murmured. He turned away and was quickly absorbed into the drift of travellers and reception parties swirling around Arrivals. Peter was relieved that the surreptitious interview was over, and stirred by the fragmentary discovery he had made.

"Peter!"

He turned immediately to the voices hailing him, and rushed forward into the welcoming crush of Konon and Leaina Konstantinou. Six years had been and gone and left their bill, but his friends looked hale and scarcely the worse for the interval.

"I've just got your message," said Konon. "You haven't been waiting too long?"

"No, not since I passed the door, and certainly not bored."

"We should think about lunch."

"Yes, preferably somewhere discreet."

Konon cast his eyes up and turned to his wife. "He's only just arrived and he's talking below-board already. All right, I know where we can stop off. Better not leave it too long; we've been waiting long enough already. The car's in the car park. Here, we'll give you a hand with that stuff."

Soon they were travelling swiftly down the straight macadam. Peter sat in front beside Konon, while Leaina, behind, talked to him over the back of his seat.

"So why haven't you gone and got yourself a wife, like a grown man?" she fussed.

"Well, you know Alice didn't want to be an Army wife," Peter smiled.

"Yes, but you left the Army."

"I did. And then I proposed to her again. And you know what? She said yes." He looked into the window of the car and seemed to see himself sneaking up behind Alice as she stood in the market place, singing Christmas carols with her parish in the nip of the Advent air. Bleak midwinter indeed, but warmed by lights, steaming drinks and cheer. Peter had slipped among the singers and caught Alice by surprise, declared his freedom and put the question again. Disarmed, she had no reason to say no. He had availed himself of the mistletoe that the occasion afforded, while the singers hailed and hooted them with mirth. She was certainly embarrassed, but had not seemed to mind.

"She said yes? So what happened?"

"Well, that was just before my accident. You can't really blame her: she thought I wasn't going to recover, and she could easily have been right. She had her own life to get on with, I suppose."

"She found someone else?" Konon inferred. "Too bad. Did she marry him?"

"Yes to the first, no to the second. But that doesn't mean that everything is sewn up. It took me a while to get back on my feet, of course, and now is decision-time."

"But there's hope?"

"Maybe," Peter said sadly. "She's supposed to be thinking it over for the last time while I'm here for a week. When I get back, I'll know how much hope there really is."

"Well, if she's got any sense we know what she'll decide," Leaina rallied.

Peter kept the reply to himself, but there, precisely, was the rub. He remembered how mortified Alice had looked, standing beside his hospital bed, as he shook his head in dismay at her distressed avowal. *Monty Breakbank? Alice! It's not that you didn't wait for me. That I can understand. It's the lapse of good taste that's hard to take.*

Konon's taste, by contrast, was unerring. It found them a restaurant, seated them outside, and chose the potent red wine which the waiter poured out for them as they perused the menu.

"So, tell me when you're ready," Konon said to Peter, once the waiter had gone back in with their order.

"Drustan McCullboy was expected here today," Peter announced. "Only he missed the flight that I was on this morning." He recounted the fruitless calls for Passenger McCullboy in Departures, and his meeting with the strange young man.

Not everything was accounted for to Konon's satisfaction. "He missed his flight? After checking in his luggage? Not what you'd expect from a professional."

"Sudden indisposition?" Peter conjectured. "Unexpected attack of food poisoning? It can happen to the best of us."

"Maybe." Konon frowned. "In any case, the boy who mistook you for him was a Rusty. One of the militia. Either that, or he wanted you to think so."

"Exactly."

"But the question is," Konon went on, "at whose invitation was the gentleman coming? Do the Rusties have their own contract with him, or does it come courtesy of 'this Government'?" He stopped for a deep draught before pronouncing on the matter. "I think 'this Government' was up to her neck in it six years ago when she was a mere minister at Defence. You'll recall our pleasant audience with Her Ingratiation. She was touchy, was she not, when you mentioned the strange car in the village?"

Peter remembered.

"What time did he say the delivery would be?" Konon asked.

"Five a.m."

"He didn't say where?"

"No."

Leaina became impatient. "So what if he *had* said where it was? There's not a lot you could have done about it, is there?"

"Maybe not," Konon shrugged. "But who knows? If there were any way of getting some pictures, there'd be no harm in having the evidence on file, for when the time comes. What do you think, Peter?"

Peter laughed. "No harm, no doubt; but no chance, surely?"

"So it would seem," Konon sighed. "But in that case what *are* we going to do all week?" He had put away another glass and was helping himself to a third. Recalling that Konon was driving, Peter found this a little alarming at such an early prandial stage. He caught Leaina's eye and saw the same thought reflected in it.

"Come to think of it," Konon went on, answering his own question, "there is the Vice-President's public lecture tomorrow. *You* should go to that."

"Are *you* going?" Peter asked him.

Konon laughed. "No point! Nothing new to learn. You, on the other hand, will find it boring as hell, but instructive. The Holy Synod's hard line on the Charter will make sense to you, if it doesn't already."

Leaina nodded vehemently. "We've been Christian for two thousand years, and they're trying to make us heathen again, the bastards."

"I think you should go," Konon insisted. "Half past ten at the Ligdos Institute. That's just across the square from the Department for the Interior."

Peter shook his head, laughing. "I don't know. I'm supposed to be getting a break for a week, with important life-decisions hanging over me, and here you are wanting me to act out *Spy Monthly* one minute, and *World Government Digest* the next – or is it both at the same time?"

Konon, glass in hand, met Peter's complaint with a defiant smile. "You're here for what little England can't offer you, right? Then stop asking stupid questions and have another drink."

# I.3. The Negotiator

"Thank you for waiting, Monsignor Longhand. The Nuncio will see you now."

Ralph Longhand rose in response to the summons, and stepped into the office of the papal Nuncio to Sardoniki. The room was comfortable and low-lit. As Ralph entered, the purpureal figure of Archbishop Fergal Shenanigan rose to meet him.

"Welcome back, Monsignor," said the Nuncio. "How was your journey? Were you on time for the Divine Liturgy at the Cathedral on your way here?"

"Yes, I was," Ralph replied. "As finely sung as I've ever heard it."

"Yes, Monsignor, I thought it would be to your taste," the prelate nodded. "How long is it since you were here?"

"Ten years," Ralph recalled. *No less*, he thought.

"In Archbishop Malfurbo's time, then?"

"*Appunto.*"

"And you were stationed here three years?"

"Two and a half. It was a good time to be here. Quiet." Ralph had indeed arrived at a moment when the Nation State Party governed, three years after a reform of the Constitution and two years after the creation of the Court of Inspection, to whose scrutiny the Government was given over. The chief opponent of that development, one of the younger constitutional lawyers at Kratistopolis University, had by then left the country. It was a calm interval, Ralph had found, fit for making the relaxed and confident acquaintance of the capital with its culture and populations, both indigenous, whether ecclesiastical, political or popular, and exogenous, whether ambassadorial, itinerant or simply expatriate. The native, self-exiled constitutional lawyer had returned to Kratistopolis only in the last months of Ralph's assignment, the narrow temporal junction at which their paths had briefly met. He had left only a couple of months before the confrontation with Ghimir over the arming of the Rustim, by which time the returning exile was standing for Parliament. Once elected, she had occupied a post in government, and latterly the president's chair. The Social Governance Party was back in power; the lull of the Vasilissa-free years was lost, its recovery scarcely to be expected.

The Nuncio interrupted Ralph's reminiscence. "Do you like my triptych?" he asked, pointing to the artefact. Saint Dalmatios stood in the centre, bearing the symbols of his martyrdom, an arrow in his right hand and fire in his left. The left wing of the triptych (on the viewer's right) showed a house wrapped in leaping flames: the hermitage of the martyred Mother Apollonia. The opposite wing depicted Apollonia herself in the act of impaling her importunate caller. The image suggested how the Norseman might have died, with an arresting look of pained surprise as the anchoress pushed the sword hilt up to his navel.

"That *is* impressive," Ralph agreed.

"I don't think I've ever seen a better representation of Saint Dalmatios," the Nuncio continued. "And you?"

"Rarely," said Ralph. He kept to himself the memory of an even better Dalmatios, a Sardonikan icon seen unexpectedly in an English country pub two years earlier, when he was doing some parish work between diplomatic assignments. The proprietors, Alfred and Marion, had not known who the saint was, and had been strangely moved when he told them the story of the martyred bishop and his riddling prophecy. *This is quite a piece, you know*, Ralph had said to them. *One of the fourteenth-century masters, probably. If you don't mind my asking, where did you get it?*

Once more, his recollection was interrupted by the Nuncio. "What do you think the saint meant when he said *He who sleeps, let him wake up*?"

"He might have meant any number of things."

"Indeed, Monsignor, hence my question," said the Nuncio, with an odd, searching glint in his eye.

"Well," Ralph replied carefully, "there's something to be said for the view that the prophecy, if such it was, was fulfilled in the thirteenth century when King Sevastos, left for dead by the invaders, got up again and won his decisive victory."

"Decisive, maybe, but not complete," the Nuncio observed. "The Disputed Zone is the living proof. It tests each government in turn, and it's testing this one now. You, too, Monsignor, in your own way, will test this Government. Really, you've the devil's own job, trying to negotiate between the Holy Synod and her."

"The devil's? I'd have said Hercules. In the stables."

"In that case, Monsignor," said the Nuncio gravely, "you'd better bring a very large shovel." He paused for a moment, then went on: "You know, it's a wonder that the separated brethren accepted a Holy See negotiator. It's certain that you won't find them very tractable."

"Who can blame them? They know what a Yes vote will mean, if the Government ratifies that Charter without excluding Article 6."

"True enough," the Nuncio agreed. "Right now, the Government of Troldhøj is seeking to outlaw the Catholic Church in its jurisdiction for not complying with statutory gender-ratio employment targets."

"How much of the population of Troldhøj is Catholic?"

"Around 0.25%."

Ralph nodded. "There's also *Pookhaggler versus Wasp*."

"I'm not sure I'm familiar with that one."

"The woman who married her orang-utan on a yacht off Costa Rica, and is now suing the State of Texas to make it recognize the union."

"Surely that's not going anywhere, is it?"

"Only slowly," Ralph conceded. "Lawyers for the orang-utan are filing for divorce."

The Nuncio frowned. "But what the separated brother bishops have to realize, Monsignor, is that the momentum of these international instruments is unstoppable. Their people won't hold out indefinitely against the lure of being modern and in line with their neighbours. If you can convince them to drop their objection to the Charter, provided that the Government vetoes Article 6, that's their best chance of avoiding the worst. Otherwise, they'll be crushed. They must negotiate now while they have the chance."

"That, of course," Ralph observed, "means getting the Government to change the terms of the referendum. Instead of Yes or No to the Charter, it would be Yes or No to the Charter minus Article 6."

"As I said, Monsignor," replied the Nuncio, "you, in your own way, will have to test the Government of Sardoniki. One thing that may help, although it is somewhat double-edged, is the old rivalry between Kratistopolis and Erithia. If Archbishop Theodoulos won't drop his opposition to the Charter in exchange for the removal of Article 6, the Bishop of Erithia might break ranks. And if that happens, Erithia just might bring Eftropos with it. Eftropos has always wheeled in the orbit of Erithia, of course. But if that happens, you'll have to persuade Theodoulos to shift, because if this Government sees the separated brother bishops divided, she'll trample all over them."

Ralph shook his head. "And how easy is it going to be, getting the old man to defer to his historic rival at the behest of the Roman negotiator?"

"*Easy* was never part of the proposition, Monsignor," replied the Nuncio wistfully. "That is what you'll have to do, or else your project fails, shovel or no shovel. Meanwhile," he added, with new vigour, "I've invited someone to join us. Someone who is now senior in Archbishop Theodoulos's clergy: Father Papias. Do you know him?"

"Not well."

"He's always happy to share things with us."

"Meaning that he's indiscreet," Ralph wanted to know, "or that he tells us exactly what His Beatitude wants us to hear?"

The Nuncio paused, his hand resting on his desk phone. "That's what you'll have to decide, Monsignor, when our guest is with us." He lifted the handset. "Ask Father Papias to come in now, please."

The quick eyes and thick beard that entered the room announced a disarming guest who laughed readily and broadly, but Ralph was soon aware of the sharp mind cogitating behind the genial mien. Father Papias was especially complimentary to him, conveying the thanks of the Holy Synod, assuring him of its determination, anticipating the discomfiture of the Government.

"A united front on your part will hardly fail to impress them," said Ralph. As he looked for a reaction, he was aware of the Nuncio beadily watching them both.

"Of course, of course, united as always!" grinned Father Papias. He glanced from Ralph to the Nuncio with a sparkle in his eye that just might have been doing duty for a wink.

Ralph threw out a question. "How do I get into the Government's mind, find out how far she might be willing to come to terms with you?"

"Ask her!" Papias replied, laughing.

"Short of getting a private audience," said Ralph, "there must be finger ends within reach who know what the brain is thinking."

"The finger ends," said Father Papias, "extend to a club called the Symposion. You know where that is?"

"Of course."

"Get yourself introduced there, if you can. You'll pick up all sorts of things, better than what they'll tell you at the Department. I've never been there, of course: it's not exactly our milieu. And there's one other thing," said Papias, lowering his voice. Ralph reflected that the hush served no other purpose than dramatic effect. There was no one in the room but the three of them, and if others were listening, a little lowering of the voice would hardly hinder them.

"Mr Secretary of State for the Interior," Papias went on, "has not had our negotiations as high on his priority list as the civil servants would like us to think. For them, it's business as usual, but it's obvious to us that Mr Secretary has not been giving it his personal attention. There are rumours that some kind of shift in military policy is keeping the whole Cabinet busy. It would be useful to know. If you ask, they won't tell you, but if you keep your ear to the ground you might hear something that would explain a lot."

The Nuncio thanked the visitor for his help. Asked by Father Papias about his plans for the day, Ralph replied that he had an appointment at the Department for the Interior.

"Then you'll be meeting Vassos Varvaros," Papias told him. "A man who's no good at hiding that he's mad at you, but he is good at carrying on as if you hadn't noticed."

"So the more I pretend not to notice, the better he'll like it?"

"Usually. Except when he wants you to get mad back at him."

"Which is precisely what I mustn't do, of course."

Papias grinned. "Play it by ear!"

"Well, Monsignor," the Nuncio asked Ralph, when the visitor had gone, "what was your assessment?"

Ralph thought. "He certainly knows more than he's telling us. But he is friendly, and he might tell us more. But he's far too much of an artist to tell us everything at once."

The Nuncio nodded. "Have a care, Monsignor. You and I are diplomats. The separated brother bishops and their clergy are not."

"I'd say this one could throw his weight with the best of them."

"As I said, Monsignor," the Nuncio repeated, "have a care."

Ralph went on foot to the Department for the Interior. There Vasilissa had begun her career as a government minister, before moving to Defence. Vasilissa had risen, and Ralph himself? He had rolled on, gaining revolutions but no ascent or descent, turning from one grinding charter negotiation to another: Civitapazza, Scammingdon, now Urkundendorf, albeit a long way from that charter's native place. When he saw it in that comfortless light, he could well forgo the tedium, wishing rather to be released, perhaps to teach canon law somewhere, perhaps to return to his diocese of Slightfield (long left behind except for the occasional visit on supply) where he could simply do priestly things. There was always the marriage tribunal. (His uncle Reginald, who had been Chancellor of the diocese, had approved the practical value of his studying canon law. As long as there were nullity suits, there would always be a bishop who would give you work.) And yet – the tension of the negotiation room still had the power to hold him, to engage him with the tenacity that the hour required, when everything, humanly speaking, depended on him and (something he missed on this singular assignment) his team. But when the hour had passed, the room would be vacated, the tension resolve itself back into tedium, and the waiting grind on.

A lean, dark-headed man was standing on the square by the Ligdos Institute, speaking to a proffered microphone before a camera. Ralph caught some of the dialogue as he came alongside them.

"Why are you expecting a statement from the Government today about the Autonomist question?"

"Because this afternoon the President will announce new plans for the security of the Disputed Zone. This will inevitably affect the Rustim lands. The question is whether the Government is now closer to granting the autonomy that we demand, or backing off from it."

Passing them by, Ralph presented himself at the Department offices and asked for Vassos Varvaros. Within minutes the civil servant appeared, alternately frowning and smiling in such a way that it was hard to say which expression was the more disturbing. He ushered Ralph into his office and provided him with a pass. Busying to and fro, Varvaros threw out remarks about the negotiations, which were to begin the next morning.

"We're grateful to the Holy See for offering to help us," he said politely. "Our Orthodox Church just has to learn that it can't get in the way of progress forever, you understand."

"Thank you," Ralph nodded. "At the same time, the Holy Synod has concerns with which we sympathize. We trust that the Government will show the necessary flexibility."

Varvaros scowled suddenly. "Hardly a unilateral requirement, Monsignor."

"Of course," said Ralph. "That was understood. By the way," he angled, "is there some kind of statement on security expected today?"

"Yes, yes, I have a security briefing for you right here," Varvaros replied quickly. "The Vice-President's lecture tomorrow is just across the square, you know. They're expecting a large turn-out. From the demonstrators, that is."

"Thank you," said Ralph, taking the briefing from the civil servant's fingers. "Actually, I meant some statement in Parliament on national or regional security. Is anything like that due today?"

"Perhaps," said Varvaros, frowning again. "Is that what the press is saying?"

"It's what someone was telling the TV cameras as I crossed the square. One of your Rustim Autonomists: their parliamentary representative, perhaps?"

"Parliamentary representative!" growled Varvaros. "They've got a nerve. Playing at being peaceful, democratic participants like everyone else, when everybody knows they're just the political wing of an illegal militia."

"But one which has the usefulness of keeping the Haman in check."

"Illegal militia are illegal militia, Monsignor," Varvaros said gravely.

"But one illegal militia is not the other. Anyway, the Autonomist said he was expecting something. It's bound to be interesting. Is it possible to see what's happening in the Chamber?"

The question had clearly taken Varvaros by surprise. "We could watch it live here in my office, if you like," he suggested.

"Thanks, but I was wondering if I might go to the Chamber," said Ralph. "Since we're so close, it seems a pity to miss the opportunity."

"Why, yes. Yes, of course," Varvaros replied, frowning again. "Just go the Chamber and present your pass, and you'll be admitted to the Observers' Gallery."

Ralph thanked him kindly, and, as soon as courtesy allowed, went on his way.

Crossing a courtyard, he passed the armed police at the entrance, went through security and up in the lift to a carpeted corridor, where a door gave access to the Parliamentary Chamber. A guard met him at the door, and opened it for him.

He walked through, into the storm.

# I.4. The Autonomists

Tishrab hurried to the city from the airport and rushed across town, fretting as he went.

First he had been disconcerted by McCullboy's unexpected behaviour. Then he feared he would be late for the Khan's interview on the square near Parliament, and, worse, for the promised showdown with the President.

When he reached the square, he saw a television crew talking among themselves, but no sign of the Khan. Annoyed that he had missed the interview, he raced on to Parliament, hoping that the confrontation had not yet begun, or at least that he had not lost too much of it. Once inside, he hastened to the Chamber, stumbling into a seat in the gallery for parliamentary staff. The Press Gallery was well filled, and there were even one or two figures in the Observers' Gallery, including what looked like a Latin priest in a black suit and white cloth collar.

The President was in her place on the raised platform faced by the rows of representatives in the semicircular Chamber. Behind her was a door opening onto a passage, known as "the Eunuch Run," by which staff members came and went on errands between the Chamber and the Office of the President. In the front rows sat the representatives from the ruling Social Governance Party; behind them, members of the Nation State Party and the Sardonikan Patriotic League. On the very last row sat Tishrab's chief, Khasra Khan, the leader and sole parliamentary seat-holder of the Rustim Autonomist Party.

"That is why," the President was saying, "this Government has concluded terms with our Convention partners to ensure the necessary security measures in the Disputed Zone. This framework will constitute the prevailing legal conditions for the maintenance of security in the Zone until further notice."

The leader of the Patriotic League leaped into protest. "This is completely unacceptable. The Government is turning the Disputed Zone into little more than a WIASCO protectorate run by a borderless bureaucracy with nothing to lose, no loyalty to our national interest, and no accountability to this assembly!"

The Chamber was filled with the audible yawns of the Social Governance Party and the agitated murmur of the Opposition. The leader of the Nation State Party sat with a look of horrified impotence. Then, deciding that he was obliged to say something, he rose and said: "It is no small irony that on the feast day of the spiritual father of this nation, the Government should choose to compromise national sovereignty by selling off its control over our territory."

Vasilissa did not trouble to reply in person, but glanced at the Secretary of State for the Interior. He spoke. "The Esteemed Leader of the Nation State Party will recall that Article 5 of the Convention regulates intergovernmental collaboration to ensure security, including domestic security, among signatories. When we ratified the Convention – in the national interest – we accepted, in principle, the assistance of our WIASCO partners to *maintain* control."

The leader of the Patriotic League intervened again. "When the Esteemed President's predecessor signed up to the Convention, that is exactly when he sold our rights to the phantom bureaucrats who will now be responsible for the most pressing area of defence policy facing this Parliament!"

Tishrab watched and listened with too much nervous excitement to follow every detail of the arguments. He wished that the Chief would intervene, according to plan. He was not disappointed. Khasra Khan rose and cast his fulgent glance across the Chamber.

"The President has now made it perfectly plain," he said coherently, but with obvious fury, "that she is prepared to contradict in public what she has been promising in private since she took office. All her *assurances* that the cause of Rustim autonomy would be advanced in the present Parliament were words, words, worthless words! When the President was a minister in the Defence Department, the Government had no difficulty partitioning the Zone. The buffer strip created on that occasion cut across our Rustim territory to the north, and Haman territory to the south. It was very simple. Where is the difficulty, Madam President, in giving autonomy to the north? I can give the Esteemed Representatives date, time and place for every one of the President's assertions that there was *no* difficulty, and that progress towards that end was only a matter of time. But now that the President lacks the will – I won't say the courage – to put that proposition before Parliament, she finds it convenient to turn the Zone into a WIASCO protectorate under a no-fly order – " (Interior tried to interrupt him, but the Khan ignored his attempt) " – that shows the hollowness of her promises and the bad faith of her dealing, such that even the Esteemed Mr Secretary could hardly mistake it!"

The Social Governance representatives were incensed. Tishrab glanced at the opposition parties and saw them caught between their thrill at the Khan's attack and their obvious distaste for the cause of Rustim autonomy which fuelled it.

Vasilissa looked across the Chamber with a tempest on her brows. "If the Esteemed Leader of the Rustim Autonomist Party is looking for sympathy in this assembly, he will find little if he proceeds by divulging private conversations where expression was free, but nobody was bound."

Uncowed, Khasra Khan continued his offensive. He even left his place and stalked across the floor of the Chamber towards the President's dais.

"I'm put in mind of a parable," he declaimed. "A parable of a dishonest marketwife. Always promising her wares and not delivering, losing credit as she abused trust!"

Before the Khan had even spoken, the impropriety that he had committed by his movements ought to have been duly corrected. The

President should have prompted the eldest representative to invite the Esteemed Party Leader to return to his place. But Vasilissa made no sign to the most venerable of the representatives. Instead, she quickly sent one of the "eunuchs" to the Chamber ushers standing at the Great Doors. At once two ushers walked across to Khasra Khan and attempted to escort him back to his place. Spurning them fiercely, the Khan cursed and hurtled in rage out of the Chamber.

The assembly was in uproar. Tishrab clutched his hand to his mouth, as if to stop his heart falling out of it and dropping onto the representatives below him. The journalists in the Press Gallery rushed down into the lobby. Tishrab, too, left his seat, and hurried out of his gallery to find his colleagues.

In the party's parliamentary office, Tishrab found Mazil, the Khan's senior adviser, watching events in the Chamber on his monitor. They looked at each other, Tishrab with wheeling eyes, the older man with sour resignation. There was nothing to be said. When the Chief arrived, there would be everything to say.

Soon enough, the Khan came clattering into the office. "Tishrab!" he shouted. "Mazil! Get the hell out before anyone gets here. Out now! Lock the door and catch up with me."

"Where?" Mazil wanted to know.

"Riverside!" the Khan cried as he flew out and disappeared ahead of an approaching clamour. Tishrab and Mazil exchanged glances again. There was nothing to be done but follow.

So it was that Tishrab found himself on the riverbank in the early evening, sitting at an outdoor restaurant table with Mazil and Khasra Khan. His sentiments wavered between excitement at what had passed in Parliament and his mounting apprehension. Nevertheless, his admiration for Khasra Khan was immense. The Chief was not only a great statesman and orator, but a war hero. When their enemy Kalgan of Ghimir, the principal prop of the Haman militia, had invaded Krastina, Khasra Khan had gone to fight against him. He had distinguished himself in the guerilla warfare until the intervention of WIASCO forces had somewhat restricted his freedom of action. He had therefore returned home with honour but without success. Now the Khan was marginalized in his own land, thanks to the Government's pact with the same WIASCO powers, and his grim mood hung over his followers.

"I've done my best," the Khan protested, "to play by the rules: open, fair parliamentary means. There's no more mileage down that road, gentlemen. It's the end."

"So what are you going to do?" Mazil asked pertinently. Mazil had been around for a long time, having been the right hand of the elder Khan before the latter's retirement from politics. The younger Khan had retained Mazil's services, but never showed him the kind of deference that his father had.

"I'm going to bring her down!" Khasra Khan declared. Tishrab started, jolted upright by a sudden thrill of scared excitement.

"I think it's time the Court of Inspection was told who's illegally supplying arms to our militia," the Khan confided. "I have an inside eye – we'll call him the Cyclops – that sees who is overseeing the deliveries. I have other eyes, too, that have seen the same person meeting Defence Department officials, and have brought me the pictures. And I have eyes at the airport. Tishrab! Did you meet Mr McCullboy when he arrived?"

Tishrab opened his mouth without really knowing what he was going to say.

"Did you meet him off the plane?" the Khan persisted.

"I met him," Tishrab said nervously.

"And did he confirm the delivery for tomorrow?"

"He wouldn't confirm anything," Tishrab confessed. "I'm not sure he trusted me. Something was making him nervous. But he's here. So there's been no change. As far as we know."

Khasra Khan frowned. "That's not good. If McCullboy suspects something, he might change the date. One moment." He switched on his phone and started searching for messages.

Mazil cast a sharp glance first at Tishrab, then at their leader. "What I think – "

The Khan cut him off with a raised hand. "Just give me a minute. There. Yes. All confirmed." He turned the phone off again. "Five o'clock tomorrow morning, then."

"The Cyclops?" Mazil guessed, the ice-peak of his irony just perceptible at the surface. The Khan was undeterred.

"The Cyclops," he averred. "A round eye, and it records what it sees. Tomorrow there should be footage, with a face in the recording to match the one in the photographs."

"And with this, you're going to betray our militia?"

"What do you mean, *betray*?" By doing what needs to be done, for their sake as much as anyone else's? Besides, accepting weapons from the Government doesn't make the militia any more illegal than it is already. It's the Government that commits the offence of supplying. She's the one who would take the consequences."

"Granted that the Court of Inspection is not in her pocket," Mazil countered, "are you sure they'd have the nerve to proceed against her?"

Khasra Khan had thought of that, too. "If we generate a little publicity beforehand, I think the momentum might be in our favour. Tomorrow morning Tishrab and I are having breakfast with the Editor of *Dikaiopolis*."

Mazil began to protest, but the Khan anticipated the objection.

"Yes, I know who owns that newspaper, and I don't care. They will run with this, that's all that matters. Tomorrow we'll get the Editor to bite, and the rest will follow. What do you say, Tishrab?"

Once again, Tishrab did not really know what to answer. It pleased him that he was wanted at the meeting with the Editor, for the Khan's plan had a rousing boldness, but the height to which it aspired was a formidably vertiginous prospect. It was a leap into the chaos of contingency, a free fall with uncontrollable consequences. A felicitous cat-landing was possible, but so was a blundering plunge into failure, setback, peril or worse. He was loath to miss it, yet eager to be spared a calamitous sequel. What, indeed, could he answer?

"You lead the way, O Khan!" was all he said.

# II. TUESDAY

# II.1. The Proprietor

"I'm sorry, Mr Aigagros," said the nurse. "Mr Ben Ezra is taking his bath at the moment."

Laios Aigagros, Editor of *Dikaiopolis*, had come all the way across town to see the newspaper's owner. The journey had taken him almost an hour. Waiting until the old man had come out of the bath could take at least as long again. The whole morning, then, would disappear, so that lunch would follow breakfast with nothing achieved in between save yes or no on the part of the Proprietor. But Laios dared not proceed without that word. Even if he had felt it safe to decide for himself, he would scarcely have known which way to choose. As a hack, he wanted the scoop. As a self-preservationist, he had no less of an investment in keeping the knock from the door, or missiles from the roof. He stood in wretched agitation, pained by the delay, seeking a way at least to shorten his ordeal.

"Do you think you could tell him I'm here to see him?" he asked the nurse. "Please. It's very important."

The nurse frowned at him, as if he did not know that bathtime was sacrosanct. Nevertheless, she nodded, saying that she would tell him, and turned towards the staircase.

Distracted for a moment from his fingernails, Laios's eyes rose and, their interest piqued, followed the nurse as she crossed the room. Disconcertingly (for there was no way she could have observed him), she suddenly stopped, turned on her heel and called out: "Is there anything else I should tell him?"

Laios mumbled haltingly that there was nothing else, thank you very much. The nurse nodded briefly, then turned back again and ascended the stairs. From under a chair, the Proprietor's tabby cat, Opsiva, fixed Laios with a green glint of inquisitorial eyes. When the cauldron of his emotions had been stirred for another twenty minutes, Laios heard footsteps on the stairs. This time it was not the sharp tap

47

of the nurse's heels, but a slower tread, creaking and ponderous. He looked up to see the old man coming down in his bathrobe to meet him.

Lazaros Ben Ezra greeted Laios with collegial cheer, and, pausing only to show Opsiva the expected paternal solicitude, insisted that the Editor sit down while he poured him a drink. When Laios had sipped a little fortitude, he expounded his dilemma. He had just had breakfast with Khasra Khan, leader of the Rustim Autonomist Party, who had claimed to have evidence that the Government was supplying arms to the Rustim militia in violation of Paragraph 13. The Khan had shown him photographs of Defence Department personnel meeting a man whom the Khan alleged to be the overseer of the arms deliveries. What was more, the Khan claimed that a further delivery had been planned for five o'clock that morning, and that he had an agent on the inside, a man of principle who was sick of the terror and extortion with which the militia tyrannized over the Rustim civilian population. This honourable man ("the Cyclops," as the Khan called him) was to have recorded the arms delivery and was willing to pass the data to any newspaper of the Khan's recommendation. That gentleman was therefore proposing to take a reporter of Laios's choice to a rendezvous with the Cyclops, say on Thursday morning, providing what would surely be the most momentous exclusive of the decade.

"Yes," said Lazaros Ben Ezra. "Yes, it would be."

The Editor's face shook with consternation. "But it could bring down the Government."

"Good," said the Proprietor. "She deserves it."

"But the last time a government got caught doing this," Laios reminded him, "there was nearly war."

"There's always war in that building," said the old man. "That's what people go into it for."

"No, no," Laios protested. "I mean war, real war! With Ghimir. Ten years ago it was that close."

"So why wasn't there a war last time?"

"Because the government fell."

"So what are you worried about? Send your people along. It'll be the story of the decade, just as you say. I have every confidence in you!"

"But why does the Khan want to involve us?" Laios persisted. "Why doesn't he go straight to the Court of Inspection? No, he wants press coverage first. He wants a scandal. It's rather unlikely to be a coincidence that this comes exactly one day after he made a scene in the Chamber because the new security plan for the Disputed Zone doesn't deliver for him. No, I don't trust him any further than the end of my nose, and I don't much care to dance on strings that are being pulled by him. You see what I mean?"

Lazaros Ben Ezra looked serenely back at him. "Son," he said patiently, "there's no need to be alarmed because the gentleman has questionable motives. It's written in the Law that the inclination of man's heart is evil from his youth. Your job is to publish what's in the public interest. Now if the Government is treating the rule of law with contempt, I think the public has an interest in knowing what she's up to, don't you?"

"Yes, but – "

"As for the Court of Inspection, they'll know all about it once you run it on the front page, won't they? Of course, when they call you up to demand the evidence, you'll let them have it, by all means. With pleasure."

Laios looked desperately down to the bottom of his now-empty glass. The old man had drained him of his objections, leaving him a hollow vessel of foreboding with nothing left to show for his disquiet.

"You have some top people to send?" the owner went on.

"Of course," Laios replied wearily.

"There you are!" Ben Ezra exclaimed proudly. "I told you I have every confidence in you. Get on the story, son." And he pointed theatrically towards the door.

Laios rose, still woefully afraid, and found himself unsteady on his feet. Lazaros Ben Ezra noticed the empty glass and asked him apologetically if he wanted another one. Laios said thanks but no, since it was still a little early. He left the house no happier than he had come, except for the cold consolation of knowing the score. *Una salus victis nullam sperare salutem.*

More than an hour later, Laios arrived back at his office. It was already past eleven thirty, and the cause of getting other business done that morning was quite lost. His secretary, Aspasia, busily prepared coffee, waiting for Laios to sit down before asking what the Proprietor had said.

"We're going to have the story of the decade!" Laios exclaimed. "The old man told me to go for it."

"Has he talked to the lawyers?"

"What do you think?" the Editor retorted. "Anyway, we won't have anything to run past them before Thursday, if at all."

"Are you going to wait until you've heard from your sources, or are you sending some of the kids along?"

"I have my orders!" he declared, breaking into an imitation of the Proprietor. "*Send your top people, son! I have every confidence in you.*"

"So?" Aspasia smiled.

"So," Laios echoed, "you know who to call."

# II.2. The Correspondent

As Ralph made his way again to the Department for the Interior, the square in front of the Ligdos Institute was packed. Not far from the main entrance stood some four hundred nationalists, the flesh-filling in a steel sandwich of armed policemen. On one side, the armoured line kept them apart from a thousand members of Militprol, who stamped around, whooping and screaming across the square. Meanwhile, people arriving for the Vice-President's lecture were grimly shuffling through an ill-organized queue at the security check.

"Monsignor!"

Turning towards the voice that hailed him, Ralph saw a quick-eyed girl with a straight regard and a confident smile, which reproduced in miniature on the journalist's badge she wore clipped onto her breast pocket.

"You're Monsignor Longhand, the Holy See negotiator?"

He acknowledged her approach, and waited for her to introduce herself as Maria Kalimithea of *Dikaiopolis*.

"Are you expecting a break in the impasse between the Holy Synod and the Government?" the girl asked with mild solicitude. Ralph saw a nimble mind at work, and liked her, but he was determined to keep his book closed to her.

"I'm sorry," he said, "but the proceedings are entirely confidential. I'm afraid you'll have to wait for a press briefing."

The journalist looked sweetly doleful. "And that could take quite some time?"

"You could ask the Department staff."

"Oh, but they already know when it's coming out." He waited for the punchline. "In due course," she said, with an exquisite hint of mockery. Ralph found himself caught between sympathy and irritation. She would have been but a schoolgirl when he was last in this city. It was time to close the conversation.

"I'm sorry, Miss Kalimithea, but you must talk to the Department staff or to the Holy Synod, or you'll have no story. If you'll excuse me," he said in parting, turning back towards the Department. Realizing that he did not really feel like going in, he paused and looked back at the journalist. "Anyway," he said, "the Vice-President's lecture's just across the square. Aren't you stopping off there?"

Her eyes laughed back. "Oh, I've already written his script," she assured him. "I'm only going to see what order he puts the paragraphs in."

"Let's hope there are no surprises."

The journalist shook her head. "I don't think I'll have any more of those than you will."

"We'll see." He turned once again and went to the Department.

In the conference room he found Vassos Varvaros with five of the Sardonikan clergy. Father Grigorios, the delegate of Archbishop Theodoulos, was already known to Ralph. They had got on well enough in more relaxed days, but it quickly became clear that Ralph could expect no favours. The representatives of the other four bishops all cultivated a disapproving look for Vassos Varvaros, a cautious glance for their leader, Father Grigorios, and a frown of high irritation for Ralph himself.

Vassos Varvaros began. "Fathers, I'm grateful to Archbishop Theodoulos and to all the bishops of the Holy Synod for their willing acceptance of the Holy See's proposal to send Monsignor Ralph Longhand as Special Negotiator."

Father Grigorios was amused. "You can bring anyone you like, Mr Facilitator. I just hope you won't be wasting the good Monsignor's time, because if you're going to repeat the same performance, we'll have to give you the same review, if you understand me."

Varvaros barely restrained himself. "Reverend delegates, it is you who will be wasting the Special Negotiator's time if you won't at least be flexible enough to listen to his contribution."

Father Grigorios almost winked at his entourage. "Mr Facilitator, who said we're not prepared to listen? But you're insisting that we swallow the Charter whole. We're having none of it. If the good Monsignor can extract you from your unfortunate position, good luck to him, and so much the better for you. But if things are as they were, I doubt it." The other Fathers nodded emphatically.

Ralph intervened. "Let me propose an hypothesis," he said to Grigorios. "You say that the Government wants you to swallow the Charter whole. Now what if Mr Facilitator here were simply to force it down your throat? Which part would you cough up first?"

The priests chuckled. One said: "I think we'd all eject it pretty much as it had come!"

Ralph persisted. "But it's too big. You can't spit it out all at once. The most disagreeable part has to come first. Which is it?"

Grigorios began to look a little suspicious, but he answered the question. "On the one hand, there is Article 2 – " he began.

Vassos Varvaros shook his head. "This is an Orthodox country," he laboured. "It's out of the question that the Government should ever try to interpret Article 2 contrary to the holy canons."

Father Grigorios parried at once. "*If* we grant that," he insisted, "there remains, as I was about to say, Article 6, which the holy canons also – "

"Which does no more than confirm existing discrimination law," sighed Varvaros.

Ralph raised his voice above the others as they burst into protest. "Mr Facilitator," he emphasized, "the Holy See is not unsympathetic to the concerns of the Holy Synod on precisely that point. It's easy to understand that the Fathers, and the bishops they represent, want a trustworthy guarantee. Granted that this Government is acting in complete good faith, a future administration, not to mention the courts, might be less respectful of the Church's norms. The Government, of course, is responsible for its own actions, but what happens in court is beyond its control. Now my proposal – ” He paused, making sure that he had got them in suspense.

"Yes?" Varvaros hissed.

" – is as follows. Mr Facilitator, the Holy Synod can't live with Article 6. You, by your own admission, can live without it."

Varvaros jumped up. "I made no admission of the kind, Monsignor Longhand! On the contrary, I said that Article 6 corresponds to existing law."

"Which exists independently of it," Ralph observed. "Mr Facilitator, since the Government wants the Holy Synod to drop its No position on the referendum, why not make it as easy as possible for the bishops to do that, by a simple modification of the terms? Instead of asking the people to approve incorporation of the Charter, ask them to approve the Charter minus Article 6."

The clergy were taken by surprise, and began to dart questioning glances from one to another. Varvaros was greatly vexed. "Monsignor Longhand, on what authority is the Government to alter the terms of the Charter?"

Ralph smiled benignly. "On its own authority. This is a sovereign state, is it not? What you incorporate into national law is entirely your own affair. Isn't that right?"

Vassos Varvaros continued to frown. "I'm afraid that the International Compliance Commission won't like the idea one bit."

"But what matters to us now," Ralph countered, looking steadily at the delegates, "is that the Government is willing to consider it. The Holy Synod is asking for this concession, is it not?"

Father Grigorios opened his mouth, closed it, opened it again quickly and said pointedly, to Varvaros: "By all means let the Government be *flexible*. We, too, will *consider* the implications of a change in the terms." The other priests nodded and spoke in support of him. Vassos Varvaros looked back at them cloudily.

"I think," he said slowly, "that our session will have to end here. The proposal must, of course, be put to the Secretary of State. In the meantime, reverend delegates, given that we are ready even to consider the Special Negotiator's proposal, I expect a reciprocal attitude. How we will ever get it past the Commission, I really don't know. Fathers, I trust we understand one another. Monsignor Longhand, thank you. You'll hear from me when we're ready to resume." He nodded gruffly, rose and left the room.

Father Grigorios and his team clattered out of their seats. "Would you care to explain, Monsignor?"

"I've made it stall," said Ralph, rising. "Haven't I?"

"And what happens when it starts up again?" one of the priests demanded. Ralph didn't reply, but looked carefully at the challenger, who represented the See of Erithia.

Grigorios continued: "Do you think that if they come back without Article 6 we're going to eat up all the rest like good boys?"

"If they come back without Article 6," said Ralph, "you'll have won a huge concession up front. The rest is details. That's where the real negotiation begins."

"Details? Such as Article 2, which will make the Church's privileges so minimal you'll need a microscope even to see them? No, no, Monsignor. I don't think you've really understood our position. Our answer to this abomination is No, and it's staying No, in whole or in part."

Ralph joined their movement towards the door. "Why not do exactly what you told Varvaros? Go back and consider the change in the terms, and then take a position. It doesn't have to be done this morning." They had begun to descend the stairs towards the way out. "What do you think?" he enquired directly of the delegate from Eftropos. The latter, caught off guard, looked quickly at Grigorios before replying.

"We will wait and see what the Metropolitan has to say," he said. The others nodded. Grigorios changed the subject for them.

"If you want to use well the time you've gained today, Monsignor," he said, "I suggest you go across the square and listen to the Vice-President's lecture. Since you will certainly know how to interpret him, I dare say you will find it instructive."

Ralph smiled. "I think I can count on a digest from someone who's already there."

"Field trip over field report, Monsignor," said Grigorios. "Go and hear it for yourself. It's only across the square."

Walking together through reception, they stepped out of the Department building and onto the square itself. Almost immediately, they wished they hadn't.

# II.3. The Archpundit

Like persistent insects, the Vice-President's phrases buzzed into the microphone in the auditorium of the Ligdos Institute, making graceless poetry on a monotone:

*ratification*
*next logical step*
*integration*
*administration*
*committed this country*
*ratification*
*legislation*
*signatories*
*interaction*
*negotiation*

Peter tried to force himself to pay attention. It didn't help that the person sitting next to him was so much more interesting.

When he had arrived, the queue at the security check was beginning to lose its initial approximation to good order. He ambled through the metal detector (thank God he had no metal bits as a result of his accident) and, leaving behind the jostling train of entrants, went in search of the auditorium.

The lecture theatre was on Floor 5. When Peter entered the lift he found the stages of the building designated in Levels (not Floors), numbered from 8 to 12. After several trips up and down in the lift, back and forth in corridors, and down several flights of winding stairs which seemed to lead in a different direction every time he tried them, he realized there was another lift on the opposite wing of the building. This seemed to take the passenger from Levels 9 to 15, and when the doors opened at Level 13 he found that this was equivalent to Floor 7. Once the lift had (for some reason) gone up all the way to Level 22, he went back down to Level 11 and at last found himself on Floor 5. There was still no immediate sign of the auditorium. Perplexed, he began to look around. Behind him a soft, friendly voice called out to him: "Are you lost?"

Turning, Peter saw a girl emerging from the lift. She wore a journalist's pass and was smiling reassuringly at him. Trying not to appear at a loss, he said casually: "I'm just looking for the Vice-President's lecture."

"It's to the left, through the doors, and then at the end of the corridor on the right," said the girl helpfully. "In fact, I'm on my way there myself." She began to walk with him, introducing herself as Maria Kalimithea, of *Dikaiopolis*.

"Peter Lotsmore," he said, shaking the free hand she offered him over her notepad-burdened left arm.

"And where are you from?"

"England."

"From England?" she said, breaking into an English that was fluent, but with enough of an accent to be charming. "Are you in politics?"

Alice would have said so, he thought ruefully. *If it really was for your country, Peter, fine. But not for the US and its damned foreign policy. Stuff that for a game of –*

"Actually, I'm ex-Army."

"Really? Then you don't find this sort of thing unbelievably boring?"

"It's a sort of hobby."

"A hobby?" she echoed, as they entered the auditorium. "What do you do for a day job? Or is daytime your time for hobbying?"

"My job *is* hobbying," he smiled, as they sat down. He realized with mild alarm not only how much he was enjoying her company, but how accustomed she was used to pulling pins of information like a magnet. He'd have to watch it.

So it was that he was sitting through the monotone poem of the Vice-President. The old tiredness began to press him, sending his head nodding and his thoughts swaying from one vision to another. The gaggle of reporters. The Sardonik girl delightfully filling the seat next to him. Hard faces, seasoned faces, callow faces, telegenic faces. Sailing with Alice one bright April day, wet and laughing. The pale Vice-President up on the platform, mouth moving. Snatches of the poem buzzed back into Peter's ears:

*elimination*
*discrimination*
*ratification*
*Constitution*
*obligation*
*consensus*
*stimulus*
*goals*
*ratification*

Peter was aware of Maria putting down her pen and shaking her head. "Order of paragraphs: standard," she murmured. He looked at her, uncomprehending.

"I was saying to someone a little earlier," she explained, "that the script's always the same. It's the order of paragraphs that's variable. Up to a point."

"Has it finished already?" he asked, noticing that the whole hall was beginning to break up into twos and threes and fours to chatter as the Vice-President walked away from the microphone to take a glass of water.

"It's the break before questions," said Maria. "Meanwhile, there's someone you should meet. There he is. With his wife."

Peter could see two very different figures, a few feet away from the crowd. The man had a slightly unkempt, weedy-tweedy look, while the frowning woman next to him seemed to be staring down her rather threatening nose, as a hunter might look along a shotgun at a hapless pheasant.

"That's Ektor Pampragmon," said Maria. "He has every qualification to say everything about anything. Every qualification except practice. He has a column in our rival, *Scholiastis*. Thekla (that's his wife) is on the City Council. If anyone ever takes you out to shoot you, it had better be her."

"And that's because – ?"

"You'll at least know that it's fair. It's only when she's finally blown your head off that you'll hear the end of how reasonable she's being."

Maria turned her smile on her approaching acquaintances. She introduced Peter to the couple, and the couple to him. He could tell that his name pulled a bell-rope somewhere in the pundit's mind, although the latter did not, for the moment, pursue it.

"I hope you're enjoying yourself in our city," Thekla said, in a tone deterrent of any negative answer.

"It's fascinating," Peter nodded vigorously. "Really."

Maria gestured towards the Vice-President. "What did you make of that?"

"He's clearly on edge," Ektor replied. "I think it's starting to get to him."

"What is?" Thekla queried.

"First, the scene yesterday with the Khan. It was embarrassing, but if the Vice is as smart as I've always thought he is, he'll see the way to get out of that one. You don't try to save face, you *outface*. But of course," he went on enthusiastically, "what the Khan himself should have understood – " Ektor broke off, as if distracted by something on the other side of the room.

"Yes?" Maria said eagerly.

Ektor Pampragmon did not finish his sentence. Over the public address system came the doom, first in Greek and then in English: "This is a security alert. All guests and staff must vacate the building and assemble on the square. This is a security alert. All guests and staff must leave the building immediately."

Ektor sighed. "Some oaf who's left his briefcase while he went to the bathroom. Still, no way to be sure. Better go."

They were scarcely given a choice. The mass of journalists was forced apart by security guards who hurried the Vice-President through the cleared space and out of the room. Then came the general rush through the doors towards the stairs. Peter, Maria, Ektor and Thekla were borne along with dreadful rapidity in the midst of the fleeing current. They were on the fifth floor, and the lift was barred to them. An alarm began to howl above the clamour, and the fear mounted.

"We're going to get crushed if we stay in this stampede for much longer!" Maria yelled at the others.

Peter warded off a body that crashed into him sideways. "Is there any other way out?"

"We've got the car out at the back," said Thekla. "Will they let us out that way?"

"Let them try to stop us! Where are the back doors?"

Ektor shook his head. "Not a good idea," he fretted. "This isn't the moment to be creative."

"Where are the back doors?" Peter roared.

"I don't think we can get to them until the second or third floor," Thekla gasped. "We're stuck in the crush till then."

"We should just do what everyone else is doing," Ektor protested.

"Ektor, shut up and keep your eyes open for where the other staircase begins!" Maria shouted as they bumped down to the next floor. "We need you and your car key."

On the second floor they veered sharply away from the downward stampede and clung to the wall of the corridor. Then they made a dash for the other staircase behind them, panting down two flights until they came to a fire exit. Peter pushed it open, and they ran out into the car park where Ektor's white Townraker was stationed. Maria harried the car's owner until he had put his hands on the key and opened up.

Thekla sank into the front seat next to her husband, while Peter and Maria scrambled into the back.

Since the wall behind the car park allowed no exit, Ektor swung the Townraker around the building and into the square. Police were forcing the protestors back in order to clear a way for the occupants of the building, who were spilling out in ever greater numbers, in higher and higher terror. The police line separating the nationalists from Militprol had parted before the onrush, leaving the militants free to get at the League members. Fighting had erupted in various spots between the Institute and the Department for the Interior. Police vans swept into the square, discharging more men to enter the savage chaos, aggravating the blockage of the escape route. Evacuees from the Institute began to stampede into the mêlée, their screams blaring over the impact of fists, heads, bodies, batons and shields. Peter followed Maria's finger as she pointed to where a figure in black ducked and swerved between two pockets of fighting.

"Ektor," she called out to the driver, "stop for him."

"For pity's sake, Maria!" Ektor chafed. "If we stop now we're never going to get out of here. What if they've mounted a roadblock? I had no authorization to move my car. No authorization!"

"Just stop for him, Ektor!" Maria yelled back at him. "He's important. He's a diplomat, for God's sake!"

Tutting and hissing, Ektor hurtled the Townraker across the square, cracking an expletive as a leg glanced off the bumper of his car, amid the howls of the person to whom the leg belonged. The Townraker screeched and jolted to a halt alongside the person who was the object of Maria's solicitude. Maria herself flung open the rear door next to her and shouted to the man in black to get in. As he did so, Maria moved down the back seat to make room, colliding with Peter and squeezing him against the door and window on the other side.

"Now drive!" Maria cried. The Townraker whined into motion, turning a loop and tearing out of the square, past police, protestors, militants and evacuees, through brawls and scrums and writhing clusters of limbs.

As Peter turned towards Maria in irritation, sore from the jolt she had given him, he saw the face of the person now sitting on the far side of her. The other looked back at him. A silent shock of recognition.

"I thought you might be in need of transport, Monsignor," Maria said obligingly. She introduced him: "This is Monsignor Ralph Longhand, the Holy See negotiator. Monsignor, Ektor Pampragmon and Thekla. And Peter Lotsmore."

The priest smiled, with a hint of irony, as he nodded in Peter's direction. "Yes," he said. "I've met Major Lotsmore before."

"*Major*, did you say?" Ektor called out from the front. Thekla's nose bore down on him at once as she ordered him to keep watching the road. Peter looked at the couple, then at Maria, then caught Ralph's eye as it returned from the same course. Snap.

"And you, Monsignor," Ektor went on, "is this your first time in Kratistopolis?"

"It's not, in fact," said Ralph. "I was at the nunciature for two and a half years. That was ten years ago, mind you."

"I don't recall that we met each other."

"I'm not sure that we did."

"Well, it's a pleasure."

"It's a relief. Thanks for the lift!"

Ektor drove on northward to his leafy home in still suburbia. Once inside, he began preparing lunch while Thekla kept the guests under familial supervision in the living room. There was a diversion, however, as Maria called her news editor.

"Yes, I'm fine. I'm with Ektor Pampragmon. Yes, he rescued us. He was quite a hero." She winked at Thekla.

The news editor's voice blared out of the banal magic box. "Aspasia was on the phone earlier wanting to know where you were."

"Aspasia? That means Laios is trying to get hold of me. What does he want?"

"Not really the moment to talk about it," the news editor apologized. "Keep your phone on: Aspasia's going to call you. Meanwhile, what about your story? How quickly can you get it to me?"

"I think lunch is coming soon, so it won't be this minute."

"Lunch won't be for a while," Thekla cautioned. "Ektor's only just started."

"Ssshh!" Maria hissed.

"What was that?" queried the voice.

"Never mind," Maria sang back. "It's just Thekla."

Peter observed her with amusement as Ralph Longhand took him to one side. "It's good to see you on your feet," said the priest. "You've recovered well."

"Yes," said Peter. "Thank God."

"What's brought you back here?"

Peter shrugged. "Invitation from Konon. Compulsory week away while someone makes her mind up. Personal pilgrimage. Destiny. Combination of any or all of the above."

Ralph smiled. "Motives are particular. Providence is all-inclusive. How long are you here for?"

"Till Monday. What about you?"

"As long as it takes. I doubt I'll be leaving earlier than you. On Sunday I'll say Mass at nine in the chapel of the nunciature, if that's any good to you."

"Thanks," said Peter, feeling both caught out and relieved, for he had not yet ascertained where he would find a Catholic Mass on Sunday. "You're working, then, I take it?"

"I'm afraid so," said the priest. "Most certainly not 'between diplomatic assignments' this time." He looked across the room. Peter's eyes followed and lighted on Maria, who was standing with Thekla, looking at a row of photographs. One of them showed their hostess and her husband in evening dress and camera-ready grimaces, and, in front of them, a pair of unsmiling adolescents who looked as if they were trying pathetically to wish themselves somewhere else.

"Palmyra's now a clerk to the International Compliance Commission," said Thekla, exercising for Peter's benefit the excellent English that the whole family, no doubt, spoke, "and Marsyas is doing a second degree at Oxford. You're not an Oxford man, are you, Major – sorry, what was your name again?"

"Peter," he said, making sure to smile. Thekla kept looking at him, still expecting an answer.

"No," he admitted. "I'm a redbrick man, I'm afraid."

"Redbrick?" Thekla was stumped. "Where's that?"

"In more places than you might think," Ralph assured her.

"And after that," Peter went on, encouraged to keep the ball moving, "I was called to the bar."

Their hostess was even more perplexed. "You became a lawyer?"

"No," Peter confessed. "It was my round." He was gratified by Maria's laughter, a merriment which also momentarily caught Ralph's attention as he crossed the room to inspect the photographs. One of the pictures showed Ektor next to a man with a sickly, stubble-stretching smile. Peter saw Ralph's eye settle on it. At that moment, their host himself came in from the kitchen.

"What about turning on the television, dear?" Ektor proposed. "There might be something about what happened back there."

Thekla, having first obtained a satisfactory progress report on lunch, reached for the remote control. Ektor glanced at his guests.

"I see you're looking at the one of me with Lykos Varys," he remarked to Ralph. "My predecessor at the University, Chair of Philosophy of Law. He was Vasilissa's political mentor, you know. The one who read the atheist manifesto she had drafted and said yes, he agreed with everything she said, but she was going to have to be more subtle. Militant materialism was not the way to go. He told her she should concentrate on defining a new morality, its source being the law, of course, and then when religion opposes its own, old-world morality to the new one, when it opposes human rights recognized by the law, then you can get them. That's what he told her. And she took his advice. She was never quite so strident on the materialist question again. She was only twenty in those days. The nationalist students called her 'the Apparat-Chick.' They hated her! Still do, of course. As you'll have realized, Monsignor, she finds it expedient to put on a more Church-friendly face, but I doubt that she's really changed her mind very much."

"Quiet, Ektor!" Thekla chided. "You wanted the news on: here it is."

The lunchtime news had startling footage of the mayhem on the square. The banners of the Patriotic League were well caught on camera, illustrating the solemn announcement that a right-wing protest had quickly degenerated to violence. Five Orthodox priests could be glimpsed as a protective shield of League members closed about them, whereas a sixth figure in black narrowly failed to get behind the same human wall. This was Ralph. Peter couldn't help being amused at the priest's dismay as he caught sight of himself, in full view of the camera, pushing and weaving between skirmishes. Peter caught Maria's eye, and they both pulled a face. As to the origin of the security alert, the news coverage revealed nothing.

"Some fool who left his briefcase outside the bathroom," Ektor conjectured once again. He was promptly driven back to the kitchen until he re-emerged with the fruit of his labours. They sat down to their meal, and no one was slow to appreciate it. Maria complimented Thekla. "This is really very good," she said. "He's well trained."

"He's my husband," said their hostess.

As they took mouthfuls of the steaming lunch, Ektor continued his commentary. "Funnily enough, her grandfather, Dimitrios, was very right-wing. He was a priest, you know. Well, after the failure of the

Hot Summer Coup, half the officers behind it were found hiding out in Dimitrios's house. The government persuaded his metropolitan to order him to give them up. Well, Father Dimitrios refused. He said he wasn't going to betray them for anyone. In the end they gave themselves up rather than have a shoot-out in the priest's house. Of course, they were allowed to go into exile: the usual gentlemen's agreement when that happens. But Father Dimitrios defended them to the last."

Peter laughed. "So what went wrong?"

Thekla explained, with Ektor seconding her antiphonally:

SHE. Well, his daughter married a Communist Party officer who was later Mayor of Kratistopolis. Oh, Father Dimitrios pleaded with her not to do it. "My child, how can you give yourself to this antichrist?" But she did.

HE. She smelled no sulphur.

SHE. Only aftershave.

HE. So she didn't listen.

SHE. Well, Vasilissa was the result.

"When Vasilissa graduated," Ektor continued, "it wasn't a good time for Communists, and the advice that Lykos Varys gave her stood her in good stead. Not only on how to take on the Church. He told her, too, that there was nothing substantial to fear from the political and economic adaptations that would have to be made. In the meantime, he said, she should look to her advantage and pursue her career, in the academy and in practice. She took his advice and bided her time. For a while she provided free legal representation for members of Militprol."

"That may come back to haunt her, after this morning," Ralph remarked. The party's hosts resumed the duet.

HE. So Vasilissa went abroad.

SHE. That's when she met her husband.

HE. Her future husband. The banking overlord. Future extra-canonical husband, of course.

SHE. Her future ex-husband, canonical or not.

"Anyway," Ektor went on, "when she came back, she stood for Parliament, got elected, was appointed to the Department for the Interior and, afterwards, the Defence Department. She was defence minister when they tried to create a buffer strip inside the Disputed Zone. The Haman mined it, and almost a whole mine-clearance team was wiped out in an ambush. The British had a man on the team, if I'm not mistaken," he added, looking hard at Peter.

Peter only nodded and said, "Yes, I remember." He frowned. Something that Ektor had just said had prodded his short-term memory. He had a question to ask, but what was it? The jammed recollection, sticking just before it could surface, made his brain ache.

"Now that she's President," Ektor observed, "*that* story certainly has come back to haunt her. She's trying to play, underhand, the unplayable card, the demon variable. The Disputed Zone."

Maria chipped in. "Yes, now you were going to say something about that back at the Institute. Before we were interrupted. Something about the Autonomists?"

Peter remembered the break in the auditorium. Maria had eagerly asked "Yes?" as Ektor paused for effect. Yes, yes, that was what he wanted to ask.

"I think," he reminded Ektor, "you were going to tell us what Khasra Khan ought to have seen."

"Oh, *that*!" said Ektor excitedly, recalling the long-departed train of thought. "Yes, of course, I mean it's ridiculous for the Khan to be upset about the Disputed Zone becoming a WIASCO protectorate. Let's face it, there's no way Rustim autonomy will ever come about under the present arrangements. There are too many domestic forces pushing and pulling to allow any partitioning of the Zone to succeed. Taking the whole thing out of the national Government's hands is the prerequisite to any solution. Why don't they see that? I'll tell you why: they want autonomy on their own terms, never mind the fact that it's not to going to happen that way, and no amount of posturing is going to make it so. Now, if you put in a peacekeeping administration that bypasses the Government, as well as cutting out the Idiotic League and the Unfit State Party, then all you have to deal with are the two tribes themselves."

"And Ghimir, of course," said Thekla.

"Oh well," her husband went on, "Kalgan's days are numbered, anyway. He's the last of the petty warlords in this region waiting to be wiped off the map. It's just another example of how national government is simply not up to the job. Yes, people get upset about the expansion of supra-national structures, and no, there's nothing very inspiring in it from a sentimental point of view. I mean there's no WIASCO folk costume, or country dancing, or whatever, but, really, it's the only way. People just don't see it. Or don't want to."

Silence followed. No one reacted except Thekla. Mouth closed in prandial rumination, she was nodding emphatically.

"How did you get on today, Monsignor?" Maria asked Ralph. "Any surprises?"

"You have to answer that question first," he countered. "Did you have any surprises?"

"Speech, no. As for the break, you could say so. And you?"

"I think our experience of break-time was much the same."

Maria's eyes returned a mock-reproach. "Is that all, Monsignor? This is off the record."

"Now, Maria," he admonished, "you were not born yesterday. *A fortiori*, neither was I."

The ringing of her cell phone diverted Maria from the impasse. "That'll be Aspasia," she said. Excusing herself, she rose and lightly moved away from the table to take the call. At first, she took Peter's attention with her, but then his ear caught a question from Ralph to Ektor.

"Ektor, are you a member of the Symposion, by any chance?"

"Of course. Why?"

"Might you be able to get me in, I mean as a guest? It's been recommended to me."

"Sure. I have to go into the city tomorrow morning. Would you like to join me for a drink?"

"Depends what time. I have to wait for a call from Varvaros to find out when he needs me in at the Department."

"Fine. I'll give you my number. We'll meet whenever you like."

Peter turned away again as his eye spied Maria returning to the table, looking puzzled. "That was Laios," she said. "In person. He wants to see me first thing in the morning. There's some new story that he wants me on. Looks like I'll have to wait until tomorrow to find out more. It's obviously something big, but he wouldn't say much over the phone. Funny. He wouldn't even tell me what it is."

# III. WEDNESDAY

# III.1. The Ghost

After only two days in her new job as the President's private secretary, Anna Kolouthou was wondering how much worse things could possibly get before the weekend.

Divorced and with two teenage children to feed, educate and (up to a point) control, Anna had been forced to abandon her second degree course when her husband left to set up home with the wife of a junior colleague whom he had fired earlier the same day. Finding herself obliged to take a job, Anna had begun working at the Central Office of the Social Governance Party, where her research and administrative skills, in addition to her long-standing commitment to the Party's programme, made her *persona gratissima*, and assured her of promotion. The Foreign Secretary's wife had encouraged her to submit her CV for the position of first personal assistant to the President, a post that had suddenly and unexpectedly become vacant. As a result, Anna now found herself proud, and a little in awe, to be working directly for the leader who so fully embodied her own aspirations and ideals: Vasilissa Athemistou. Rumours of bad blood between the President and her last PA left Anna perplexed. Clearly some people, even (embarrassing though it was) some women, didn't know when they were well off.

For all her competence and commitment, Anna was nevertheless finding the first week trying beyond her apprehensions. Knowing what, or what not, to say to the President after the scene with Khasra Khan on Monday had been difficult enough. On top of that came Tuesday's bomb scare and the violence from the far-right protestors outside the Ligdos Institute. That had spun the Office of the President into a hurricane, from which Anna had gone home feeling as if she had been fed into the shredder. Now, on Wednesday morning, she was back at her desk while the President, in the Parliamentary Chamber, supported the hapless Secretary for the Interior as he fielded the missiles of hostile representatives. Anna knew she should consider herself lucky to be fielding only telephone calls, but she anticipated even that with a certain dread.

The telephone rang. Anna took the call. "Hello," said a man's voice, softly, "this is the Ghost. May I speak to the President, please?"

Anna thought that maybe she hadn't heard correctly. "I'm sorry: who did you say you were?"

"The Ghost," the caller repeated. "The Ghost in the Bathroom."

The voice was cultured, polite and friendly, but Anna thought that the courtesy overlaid something unsavoury, especially in the little chuckle that accompanied the impenetrable private joke. She forced herself to remain calm. "One moment, please," she said coolly. Putting the caller on hold, she consulted Niki, the President's other secretary. Older and unwilling to change her hours, Niki had been content to remain second personal assistant when Anna's predecessor had left.

"There's a funny call on Line One," said Anna. "It's a man calling himself – " (she paused, making sure that she wasn't making it up) " – the Ghost in the bathroom."

Niki returned a droopy nod that said she it had heard it all before. "Oh, him. That's Felix. Her ex-husband, you know."

Anna was horrified. She had had the Chief Executive of the Banking Consortium on the line, and she had put him on hold.

"It doesn't matter," Niki assured her. "Just tell him the President's in session."

Barely maintaining her composure, Anna returned to the caller on Line One and conveyed the information. "I see," said the voice. "I'm afraid it's extremely urgent. Could you have a message taken in to her?"

Anna knew that this measure was indeed possible, but severely restricted in its application. However, in view of the caller's presumption, and Niki's relaxed attitude, she inferred that the criteria were met. She agreed to take a message. The caller simply wanted the President to be told that he was on the line for her.

"By the way," he continued, "you're new, aren't you? What's your name?"

Frost formed in Anna's veins. "Mrs Kolouthou," she informed him.

"Oh," he said, with the same mocking chuckle. "Your predecessor was just Efi to me."

Anna wished she could send her breath, laced with shards of ice, down the telephone line and kill him with it instantly.

"I'm Felix," he introduced himself. "Felix Saturnian."

"Thank you, sir," Anna replied, relieved to be putting him again on hold. "He wants me to send in a message to her right now to tell her he's on the line," she told Niki.

"That's fine," said her colleague. "Just send it in with one of the eunuchs and she'll see it in no time."

Anna shook her head. Niki grinned. "It does take a little getting used to, doesn't it?"

Hardly dissenting, Anna wrote out the note. Within seconds she had given it to one of the Office staff who had access to the corridor leading to the President's chair in the Parliamentary Chamber.

Anna found out later that the intervention of the "eunuch" had, in fact, brought further embarrassment to the Secretary of State for the Interior. He had been striving to save face amid the tumult of Nation State Party and Patriotic League representatives, with the President sitting behind him in grave silence. The leader of the League was on the offensive. "Only the Esteemed Mr Secretary has made that particular allegation," he bellowed at Interior. "Mr Secretary is completely isolated!"

At this point, the Office staff member approached the President, showing her the message that Anna had written out. Signalling to the Vice-President to take over from her, Vasilissa rose quietly without announcement. Unaware of this, Interior retorted loudly to the leader of the League: "I can assure the Esteemed Party Leader that the President is right behind me!"

The general uproar told Interior that something was badly wrong. Nervously he looked back to the President herself, and found that, behind him, the chair was empty.

Meanwhile, Vasilissa was hastening back to her office suite. She burst in on Anna and said abruptly: "What line is he on?"

"Line One," Anna replied gingerly, still hoping that she had done the right thing.

Vasilissa shut her door and took the call. After ten minutes she emerged and went over to Anna.

"Did you find him a little hard to take?"

"Not particularly," Anna dissembled.

The President smiled with amused sympathy. "Don't worry," she said. "There's nothing I need to be told about him. By the way, how are you getting on? I'm sorry it's turning out to be such a hell of a week. I really haven't been looking after you properly. How is it?"

"Well," Anna began, as bravely as she could. "I'm sure it will get easier – "

Vasilissa laughed. "Don't be sure of anything," she warned. "Look, we really should have a drink before the week's out. Let's see: today it's Wednesday – what about Friday night?"

Anna smiled gratefully. "Perfect!"

The President excused herself. "I must get back to the zoo," she said. "Can't let the animals screw everything up while my back's turned."

"Good luck," Anna called after her. She returned to work with immeasurably boosted morale. It was good, she reflected, that the President had invited her for a drink before the week was out. Clearly she was not expecting things to become any more frantic in the next few days, after all.

# III.2. The Satellites

"Any the wiser as to what, exactly, happened yesterday?"

The questioner was General Leonidis; his interlocutor, Major Ravdos; the object of his enquiry, the lapse of public order outside the Ligdos Institute, and its cause. They sat in the General's office at Inner Command, close outside the city, to the south.

"*False alarm* is all anyone is saying," replied the Major, with an ambivalent manual gesture.

"The forgotten bag, then," said the General. "Much security about nothing."

"I suppose so, sir. Unless – "

"Go on."

"Unless it wasn't simply forgotten. Of course, if the bag, or whatever it was, was left there on purpose, that would mean that someone specifically wanted an evacuation onto a public square where volatile rival factions were facing each other, with only a highly disruptable police line between them."

"*Cui bono*, Major, that's the question," the General retorted as he lit a cigarette.

"Not this Government. Unless – "

Smokestream. "Go on."

"Unless the Patriotic League was to be framed for the disturbance. Otherwise, provoking unrest of that kind, in that way and under those circumstances is, as you imply, sir, more likely to be the work of someone acting against the Government than for it."

"The Khan's revenge?" The hypothesis floated upward, swirling. "But I wouldn't expect the Khan to try a trick that leaves so much to chance, would you?"

"No, sir," the Major agreed. "Another thesis would be that someone higher up than this Government has an interest in disturbing the peace that this Government is meant to be keeping. In preparation for shaking her off, for example."

Cough. "Do you think her performance to date is such a disappointment to them?"

"To all appearances, no, sir," the Major conceded. "The trouble is that *appearances* are all we have to go on." And he, too, lit up.

General Leonidis needed no lesson about appearances. His father had moved on the periphery of the circle that had initiated the Hot Summer Coup, but since he had not *appeared* to be involved, he had retained his commission after the conspirators had been summoned, hands over heads, out of the sheltering house of Father Dimitrios and into permanent exile. The younger Leonidis had followed his father's calling, and had also maintained an appearance that was nothing if not unobjectionable, so much so that he had been approved as Chief of Staff by none other than Dimitrios's own revolutionary granddaughter who was now President of the Republic of Sardoniki.

Vasilissa's sphere of law, and the General's own martial one, were satellites of the body politic that had kept their own orbits, until hers had shifted towards the centre with her rise to the Defence Department. He had noted her ascent and recognized her for what she was. Their first, brief, conjunction came with the massacre of the mine-clearance team on his watch as commander of Shield Base. The news of the ambush reported by Konon Konstantinou had taken him by sickening surprise. First, the team's transport had simply broken down. But before another vehicle could be sent, Konstantinou was back on again, howling a tale of death from the desert down the line to the base. Leonidis at once sent a helicopter, which found the immobile transport and eight dead men. Konstantinou and the British officer were missing and could not be reached, until a call came in from them as they sat in a base of the Rustim militia. When they had reached that doubtful refuge, as Leonidis learned from them on their return, misfortune's wheel had spun from the field of mere blunder to that of the undeniably suspicious. One of the Rustim had fired on them, and the Englishman had glimpsed a luxury car from Kratistopolis that his captor-hosts were at pains to keep out of his sight. A further interview with the survivors, after they had given evidence to the defence minister, revealed Vasilissa up close as he himself had not yet seen her: as an attorney, naturally enough, but acting for whom? The two officers had been interrogated as hostile witnesses, if not, indeed, as the accused. The defence minister, in whose favour the Army itself had forgone an enquiry, seemed rather to be the abortionist of the truth than its *accoucheuse*. The matter thus stifled, the movers went their way: Konon left the Army, the Englishman went home, and Vasilissa – Vasilissa rose to the presidency, so that a second conjunction occurred when his own appointment as Chief of Staff was put before her, and approved. Who indeed, with the benefit of such good fortune, would underestimate the value of appearances?

The General stubbed the remains of the weed, fierce red expiring into black smudge. The Major had not quite finished his.

Ten years earlier, when a government was caught arming the Rustim, and war with Ghimir was imminent, the general staff was divided in its sentiments. For some, defence was a duty, should the president command it; for others, such a war would be the unconscionable price to pay for misrule, to be averted, if necessary, by turning on the misrulers and swiftly removing them from office. The collapse of that government by political mechanisms did away with the dilemma. And as long as the rule of law ran straight and the democratic clock ticked and cuckooed, the dilemma hid its horns, sparing the general staff, and the Chief of Staff, the supreme conundrum. That state of affairs still *appeared* to obtain.

The telephone rang in the Major's office, adjacent to the General's. "Ravdos. Yes. Of course. Really? Since when? I see. No. No. Yes, if there's anything else. Yes. Thanks. You too."

"Anything relevant?" the General wanted to know.

"Possibly." The reply was served with precisely measured restraint. "Drustan McCullboy has been seen in town."

# III.3. The Real McCullboy

The negotiations between the Holy Synod and the Government had not yet resumed, and Ralph was waiting on Varvaros to summon him back to the table. In the meantime, he was following up the recommendation of Father Papias that he try the Symposion as a source of information. He had, of course, been a guest at several clubs in the city back in the day, but not at this one, which, as Papias had justly remarked, was not exactly a clerical milieu. Nevertheless, accompanied as he was by Ektor Pampragmon, Ralph gained immediate admission. Leaving reception, they walked up a flight of stairs to a gallery hung with operatic curtains and dominated by a mural sculpture of Prometheus. The Titan was bound to the jutting rock with manacles that seemed absurdly small on the over-muscled arms of the massive *Übermensch*. At his navel, the avenging eagle tore away sharply, its beak full of liver, while the Titan held his head up and his mouth open, rolling his eyes and screaming furiously at heaven.

Ralph and his obliging host came to a lounge, which was empty except for a staff member serving at the bar, and a member of the club whom Ralph could see in half-profile. At first glance, he thought it was Peter Lotsmore, and was about to ask him what he was doing there. It was well, however, that he refrained. When the figure moved in his seat, he could see clearly that it was not Peter Lotsmore, although the difference in build and complexion between Peter and the stranger was not great. The seated man turned towards Ralph and fixed him with a hostile stare as he stood there in his black suit and white Roman collar. Ralph looked back at the man without wavering, but without provocation, still a little surprised at the near-mistake of identity.

Another staff member entered the lounge and walked over to the seated man. Discreetly he conveyed a message to him, at which the man rose and left the room at once.

Ektor guided his guest towards the bar. "What can I get you?" he invited.

Ralph glanced at the spirits (these spirits being of a most visible kind) and hesitated. "I don't know. It's a little early."

"It's at least halfway to lunchtime," the archpundit objected, and prevailed on Ralph to join him for a whisky.

"Did you see the man who left the room?" Ralph asked as they sipped.

"Oh, him? He always comes here when he's in town."

"You know who he is?"

"Meaning that you don't? But then, why should you? He's not exactly in your field. No, that's Drustan McCullboy. Cramminghead, Cambridge, Sandhurst. Service on three continents. Left the Army and made a name for himself in GRAPSON."

"I'm sorry, where?" Ektor's last word might have suggested a literary or secretarial agency, but Ralph doubted that the referent was anything of the kind.

"*Ground–Air Precision Solutions*," Ektor explained. "Contracts in four regions, fee maximum, damage minimal. Did you know it was McCullboy who captured the President of Meerkatsmark? Air assault: that's his speciality. He landed a helicopter on the roof of the presidential palace and brought Nokandu out with no damage except a few cracks in the ceiling. Well, he broke a funeral jar that was a thousand years old, almost impossible to bid for and certainly irreplaceable. But that was the last thing anyone cared about."

Ralph recalled the events. It was certain, he reflected, that the unfortunate Balthasar Nokandu had other things to worry about than the priceless funeral jar. He had at least been spared his own funeral, for the time being.

Ektor continued his commentary. "McCullboy just left early. That says 'business.' No doubt he's on his way to meet the man from the Department."

"The Defence Department?"

"You bet!" Ektor laughed. "Security in the Disputed Zone is a tough one for any government. The services of a competent ... *consultant* are worth every obol."

"Really?" Before Ralph could elicit further information, his phone rang. It was Vassos Varvaros, telling him that the negotiations with the Holy Synod would resume in one hour. Ralph looked at his watch; he had just enough time to get there, cutting it fine. He finished his whisky, thanked his host kindly, and left the lounge. Walking past the blaspheming Titan and down the stairs, he left the club and made his way over to the Department.

The square in front of the Department was not as it had been the day before. Then, it had been packed to madness with the seething crowd. Now it was empty, save for the armed vigilance of the Municipal Police. Ralph entered the building and went to the conference room, where he found the same cast of unsmiling clerics and screen-faced civil servants. Varvaros began the new scene.

"Yesterday," he summed up, "our Special Negotiator, Monsignor Longhand, made the somewhat unusual proposal that this Government change the terms of the proposed referendum. Instead of the integral text of the Charter, we should propose the Charter minus Article 6." He paused, looking around the table to meet the interrogative glances cast his way.

"Given the considerable difficulties," he went on, "of seeking to make changes unilaterally to the text, the Department proposes, rather, a variation on the suggestion made by the Special Negotiator."

Ralph tried to not to show his irritation. His stroke of the previous day had gained some time. Now, the second edge was being whetted by the Department.

"The Department," Varvaros continued, "has drafted a protocol which states that this Government's interpretation of Article 6 is not in conflict with the holy canons. Here is the text." One of Varvaros's aides began to distribute copies to the assembled delegates, and to Ralph.

"But this is preposterous!" Grigorios objected. "It's not for her to say what's in accordance with the holy canons or not!"

"It would help," said Ralph deliberately, "if the Department were to specify in the text of the protocol that the Government recognizes the competence of the Holy Synod to determine what is, or is not, in conformity with the holy canons."

"At least!" said Grigorios, with vehemence.

"But even then," Ralph continued, "I can see a weakness in the otherwise admirable idea of the protocol, which might make its acceptance difficult for the Holy Synod."

The delegates sat up. Ralph tried not to smile. Vassos Varvaros restrained himself.

"And what is that, Monsignor?"

"Once again, the courts," said Ralph. "Unfortunately, the Government's honourable proposal is not judge-proof. Suppose the courts ruled that, in the event of a conflict between Article 6 – as interpreted, of course, by the judges – and the proposed restriction, the restriction has no force. So the Government's best intentions would be frustrated by judicial *fiat*."

"What do you suggest?" Varvaros hissed.

"Drop the Charter!" the delegates chorused. Ralph quickly intervened.

"Take out Article 6," he appealed. "Sardoniki is a sovereign state. What are the difficulties that you mentioned?"

Varvaros shook his head. "Monsignor, you don't need me to explain the delicacy of trying to justify a unilateral action of that kind to the Commission."

Ralph pressed him. "Have you tried?" The delegates scarcely concealed their amusement at the discomfort of Varvaros.

"I am not aware that Mr Secretary has been in contact with the Commission's secretariate about the matter," the Facilitator replied coldly.

Without waiting for approval from Grigorios, two of the priests called out: "Ask them! Ask them!" Ralph noted with satisfaction that they were playing his game. Interestingly, these two were not from the sees whose loyalty to the Metropolis was rumoured to be the loosest.

"Mr Facilitator," Ralph persisted, "all that is being asked is that the Government contact the Commission with this proposal."

Varvaros sighed. "Which means that now we must adjourn exactly where we left off yesterday."

Ralph smiled. "As I said, Mr Facilitator, that's all that is being asked."

# III.4. The Listener

Tishrab felt cautiously courageous as he entered the offices of the newspaper *Dikaiopolis*. Tuesday's breakfast had increased his appetite for the Khan's project, thanks largely to the latter's performance. The Chief had baited the shaggy Editor with the tale of the Rustim militia's extortions and beatings among their own people, and their cheaply chalked-up civilian casualties among the Haman. It had been an affecting testimony. Some of it was even true. The pinnacle of the Khan's piece was his keen homage to the integrity of the Cyclops, the insider willing to supply the newspaper with a recording of the latest arms delivery that would reveal its supervisor: a face in motion that would match the face in the stills.

The Editor had manifestly found it all highly exciting, but he was also hesitant, always putting questions, never committing himself. He would have to talk to the Proprietor, he had said. He would let them know once he had run it past the old man. This had lowered Tishrab's expectations, but the Khan had been more confident that the next call would be an invitation to the Editor's office. And so it was. Tishrab's morale was fanned, even more so when the Khan sent him to the meeting as his sole representative. Maybe he had a future in politics after all, despite the scepticism of his clan elders, who saw little point in his pursuing anything except livestock.

Laios Aigagros welcomed him edgily into his office, grinning and pouring rough coffee. They were soon joined by two others, whom the Editor at once introduced to his guest. One was a hardy fellow with a frank face and a bracing grip on the hand: the photographer Nikos Palinouros. The other, a reporter, was a girl about Tishrab's own age, perhaps a little older, favoured with clear skin, sleek hair and quick eyes that missed nothing: Maria Kalimithea. She crossed herself fervently in the Greek manner in front of the icon of the Theotokos that hung in the Editor's office. Like many in the Rustim political milieu, Tishrab was fairly secularized and tolerant of Christians. He was not, then, greatly disturbed by Maria's spontaneous act of iconodoulic piety, but having to interact with this scintillating person was a different matter. He broke out into a sweat as he shook her hand under double duress, both of manners and of the searching glance with which she fixed him. To the aggravation of his malaise, the Editor commenced business, saying: "Sohrab here – "

"Tishrab," he corrected him.

" – is personal assistant to Khasra Khan." Rehearsing Tuesday's tale, Laios produced, for the inspection of his two colleagues, the pictures of Defence Department staff with McCullboy that the Khan had passed to him. "Exhibit A. Now Sahib here will tell you how to come by Exhibit B."

Humming, false-starting, and rattling his coffee cup in its saucer, Tishrab put the proposition: the next morning, the journalists might accompany the Khan, Mazil and himself to Ferood's Garage outside Erimopolis in the Disputed Zone. There the Cyclops would meet them in a back room, tell his own story and hand over the recording to them. While the place of the meeting was, of course, a strict secret, the hillsides and villages would afford ample pictorial matter to illustrate an article. If they liked, of course. It was up to them.

The girl exchanged a sharp look with the photographer, then turned her glance even more sharply on the Editor. "Laios, can we have a word with you for a moment?"

She was seconded by the photographer: "In private."

Although Laios tried to gesture surreptitiously, Tishrab saw the Editor nod in his direction, embarrassed at the request for a secret audience. The journalists insisted. Ushered out of the room with all of Laios's apologetic geniality, "Tahrib" was left with cup in hand and an invitation to help himself to a refill from the coffee machine in the corridor. Dissembling a present lack of appetite for any more of the rough blend, he stayed by the machine until Laios was back inside the office and had shut the door. Making sure that he was unobserved from either end of the corridor, Tishrab crept as close as to the door as he could without being seen through its glass pane. Crouching, he listened as the coruscant girl confronted the tense satyr.

"Laios, this is one hell of a risk, do you realize that?"

"Risk? As in, political?"

"As in life-and-limb, too, Laios," the photographer interjected. "We are talking about the Disputed Zone, damn it."

The girl continued to press the Editor. "Have you spoken to the old man?"

"Yes."

"When?"

"Yesterday. At ten thirty. Any more questions?"

"What did he say?"

"He said: 'Go right ahead.' He said he had every confidence in me – in us."

"Laios, if this is really about a violation of Paragraph 13, you'd better have everything ready to hand over to the Court when they come calling. Otherwise we – you – are really going to be in for it, you know that?"

Tishrab was amused to hear her speak like that to the hairy oaf: a teacher explaining to a dull child what would happen if he tried using the sharp end of his scissors to get the attention of the boy next to him.

"Of course!" the Editor protested. "We agreed that, too. At the old man's house. What else would you expect?"

The photographer intervened again. "Look, Laios, apart from all that, there's far too much here that you're simply taking on trust. Not least the security of the rendezvous young Jitters is offering us."

"Come on, Nikos, you were in Krastina. That was much more dangerous than this."

"Maybe, maybe not. The risk assessment was easier there: that's the difference."

"Are you objecting to the assignment?"

"I'm saying we need to talk about guarantees."

Tishrab had time only to hear the girl begin to articulate her agreement before the rap of high heels announced an approach around a corner into the corridor. He sprang away from the door, taking care to stay low until he was clear of it, then seized on the alibi of the coffee machine, feigning an interest in making a selection. Aspasia, the Editor's secretary, had almost reached the office door when she saw him. She stopped, took in the sight of him, and seemed to snigger. What did she want, then? The old bag.

Aspasia clopped at the door, opened it slightly, then paused on the threshold. "Sorry, is it not a good time?"

"No, no, it's fine, Aspasia. Come in: I'll be with you in a moment." Aspasia opened the door fully as Laios turned again to the two journalists. "You'll get back to me at once? Maria?"

"Soon as I can."

"But she's right, Laios. We're not leaving it the way it is."

"All right. All right." The Editor spread helpless hands and again pulled a sweet-and-sour face as Tishrab held the empty coffee cup towards him, silently seeking a refill of explanation. "I'm sorry, Talib, there's just a little practical point to clear up before my colleagues can confirm when and where they'll meet you tomorrow morning. Wait for our call. We'll get back to you as soon as we can. Thanks for coming. Our regards to the Khan."

The editorial party resolved itself into new configurations: Laios and his secretary at the desk, the photographer and the reporter making for the door, he following her. Tishrab was left standing outside, cup still absurdly in hand. In the end it was the photographer, not yet out of the room, who relieved him of the cup and saucer, nodding politely to him before turning back and thrusting the crockery without a word into the hand of a surprised Aspasia.

Tishrab walked back down the corridor, tailing the journalists. The girl (of course) became aware of him and signalled to her colleague. The two of them stepped into the lift, the photographer saying apologetically to Tishrab: "It's a bit tight in here. Do you want to wait till it comes up again? Or take the stairs?"

Tishrab took both the hint and the stairs. He pondered what to do: tell the Khan at once, or wait for a confirmatory call, in the hope that one would come before a report became unavoidable? A middle course was perhaps the best: wait until lunchtime, no, a bit longer, until coffee time, then think about starting to make his way back to the Khan's office if he had heard nothing by then. What if *Dikaiopolis* declined the offer? It was a poor prospect for the Khan's enterprise if even the city's most anti-Government newspaper would not run with the story. The journalists' misgivings conjured up the ghost of his own apprehension. Perhaps he had been right, after all, to fear that they were all on the heady edge of an uncontrollable plunge into the abyss.

At the bottom of the stairs, he saw the lift strike bottom and disgorge its freight. He was glad, given the feeling in his stomach, that he had not taken it.

# III.5. The King

Once the Tuesday lunch party had broken up, Ektor Pampragmon had insisted on driving all three of his guests home. Ralph Longhand had disembarked first, at the door of the nunciature. Maria had got out close to her flat, while Peter, thinking it best not to mention the name of Konon Konstantinou, had asked to be taken to the Kratistopolitan Hotel. He had walked in and gone to the bar while Ektor drove on and back to suburbia. Peter had bought himself a drink and called Konon, whiling half an hour away in sipping and thinking until his host arrived to drive him home. His stomach full of Ektor's lunch, Peter had been obliged to defend himself, within the limits of guest-etiquette, against Leaina's attempt to feed him as much again. He had not done too badly, he felt. Sir Gawain himself would have been fairly stretched by such a challenge to his courtesy.

That was yesterday. Now, Peter was lounging in the Konstantinou living room as Leaina gathered ingredients in the kitchen and Konon hunted in the basement for a DVD. The unostentatious room housed an icon of the Anastasis, one or two paintings and an episodic history in photographs. Konon the young soldier. His wedding with Leaina. Their daughter who had died at the age of five. Konon and friends on holiday in the Alps. Leaina and her friends having a party at a bar. Glancing away from the pictures, Peter saw Leaina herself approaching, laden with a tray of overpowering coffee and more of her curious pastry that was syrupy to excess but strangely appetizing. These were to keep him supplied until the evening meal was ready.

Peter's phone rang. It was Maria Kalimithea. Whether he was more pleased (that she had called) than annoyed (at her for calling him, or at himself for having exchanged numbers), or more annoyed (on either count) than pleased, were alternatives that resisted analysis, even his own.

"Could we meet?" she asked him. "It's about a job."

"I don't give interviews," he parried, trying to sound facetious.

"It's not about – it's not about you. It's a tricky assignment. I might need some backup."

"All right. Can I bring a friend?"

"Sure. I'm bringing a colleague."

"Bar of the Kratistopolitan?"

"Fine. How quickly can you get there?"

"One hour?"

"Great."

"See you there."

Konon appeared, film in hand. "Got it!"

"Better save it for later. I've been called out. The girl from the paper wants backup on a job. Want to come?"

Konon considered for a moment, then nodded, impressed. "I said 'what are we going we do all week?' It looks as if you were the right man to ask. Where do we go?"

"Back to the Kratistopolitan. I told her 'in one hour.'"

"Right." Konon looked into the kitchen and hailed the housewife. "We're going out. Peter has to meet someone."

The tap was on; protest flowed simultaneously. "I can't just leave everything like this! Not if you want dinner before the evening's out."

Konon shook his head. "I said *we're* going out, not *you're* going out. See you later!"

They heard a further exclamation from the theatre of culinary operations as they slipped out of the house towards the car.

At the hotel, the introductions went as Peter had expected. Meet. Shake. Sit. Drink. Talk. But when the talking began, the proposition confounded expectation: Ferood's Garage, at nine the next morning, to watch the backs of Nikos and Maria while Khasra Khan took them inside to see the Cyclops, recorder of an arms delivery said to have taken place the previous day, supervised by Vasilissa's gun-runner.

Peter restrained himself from laughing aloud, and tried not to look amused. Had he needed a mirror, he had one in Konon Konstantinou. Eye-contact afforded the sharing of the joke and an agreement that they would take the job. More conversation established the plan: under cover of a landscape photography expedition, Peter and Konon would stop at the garage ahead of the Khan's rendezvous and ask Ferood to check some function of the car. Able thus to look and move around the place, they would give the journalists early warning, should anything warrant it.

The photographer seemed satisfied, Maria delighted. "Are you going to tell Laios, or shall I?" Nikos asked her.

"I'll call him," she said. "I promised, so I'll deliver."

"Good. I'm going to call my wife, tell her I have an early start tomorrow."

"And so do we," Konon observed, with a nod to Peter. They returned to the car.

Never had Peter had a car journey in which he or the driver (if these were not one and the same) had laughed so loud or long. "I said the time would come, didn't I?" Konon insisted. "And despite the sceptics, we do get to see it up close."

"We have front seats," Peter admitted.

"We're stage management," Konon corrected him. "In the wings. Good enough for me."

"In one way I have an advantage over you."

"That is?"

"With things ... in suspense, I'm not the one who has to sell the venture to the wife."

Leaina was indeed irritated that Konon had accepted a security job when he was supposed to be on holiday the whole week, and that he was dragging Peter along with him. She was even less in favour of it when they acknowledged the location and nature of the enterprise. On Monday, she had thought it for the best that there was nothing they could have done had they known where the arms delivery would take place, and she saw no good, and plenty of risk, in involvement after the event. But Konon would not miss it for anything, and Peter, owning that he had made a friend of Maria, felt a certain obligation in the matter.

After dinner, Konon prepared what they would need the next morning. Preferring not to wait for the pretextual check at Ferood's, he looked the car over, then assembled their equipment: cameras, binoculars, canteens, flasks, handguns. When all was done, they finally watched the film that Konon had retrieved. A work of Sardoniki's most popular Communist filmmaker, *Sevastos Wakes* was a grand caricature that transcended its ideological stamp, thanks to the exquisite genius of its cinematography. Peter soon found himself fixed to the bold monochrome montage. There was King Sevastos himself, grinning genially and sending all his court into hilarious uproar. All, that is, apart from the scheming Chancellor and Chamberlain, who skulked together, louring in the shadows at the edge of the throne-room. There was the arch-enemy, Akir the Potent, august and inscrutable as he slowly squeezed poison out of a toad. All the while he was interrogating a frightened Sardonikan peasant, who lay cowering on the floor of Akir's fluttering pavilion. The evil-eyed, brush-bearded Toadkeeper looked on from his lurking-place in the dark folds of the enemy tent.

The King's army marched south, a waving cornfield of pennants, to the roll of the drum and the swell of a deep-throated patriotic song. In the gloom of the sleeping camp, Sevastos roused his two hand-picked companions and rode off with them to reconnoitre across the plain. Daylight was spreading over the austere hills when they halted beneath the assassins' cave. Then the assassins moved, barely to be glimpsed in the terrifying speed of their strike. Sevastos, thrown from his horse, lay still in a crack in the earth, until the clear sky of day became night.

He who sleeps, let him wake up. The King stirred and struggled out of the shallow pit. Retrieving a riderless horse, he pursued the assassins and caught up with them by moonlight. His sword darted about and struck them down in a dancing *chiaroscuro* of sudden death. The two armies rose against each other in the plain before the mountains, dashing together like the collision of passing icebergs, sending splinters of fighting men into every corner of the screen. The King had the best of it, his victorious pursuit passing over the crushed bodies of the invaders until it burst into the enemy camp, where the abandoned pavilions were set alight. The fire leaped and blossomed in the desert, until the bells of Kratistopolis acclaimed the return of Sevastos in his triumph.

The light on the screen diminished and was absorbed into darkness. The night grew elderly and drowsy. Peter and Konon had an early start the next morning. Time to turn in.

# IV. THURSDAY

# IV.1. The Cyclops

Ferood's Garage stood alone on the road to Erimopolis, wild hills behind it and a rough slope opposite. The premises were basic: forecourt, workshop, office, outdoor toilet. Tyres were piled by the wall near the workshop. The tiny office gave onto a slightly larger room where the Cyclops waited. When Khasra Khan's Land Rover pulled into the forecourt, the disembarking party (Tishrab, Mazil and the two journalists) found Ferood busy about a car while its driver and passenger, two exploratory types, loitered nearby. Ferood was a quiet but friendly fellow who always fixed Tishrab's cousin's truck when it broke down, an event that occurred with a frequency that inconvenienced his cousin but was hardly without advantage for Ferood. In any case, his cousin never showed the slightest interest in acquiring a replacement truck.

After a word to Ferood, the Khan directed his party to go into and through the office. Except Tishrab. "You stay here and keep your eyes open."

"For what?"

"Those two, for example. Anything else unusual, call Mazil at once."

Tishrab frowned. If there was any danger, it would surely be safer inside. At the Khan's insistence, he carried a pistol (all three of them did), but it made him nervous. He hated the kick and bark of practice which, again, he kept up only under compulsion.

*We all sat down*, Maria testified afterwards. *The Cyclops started to play us the recording. It didn't tell me very much. Truckloads of weapons, inspection, unloading. I could see the man who was supervising it: he was supposed to be the same as the one in the photographs. I'd seen those pictures, but I'd have had to put them together with the film to be sure. The quality wasn't all that good.*

One of the two men by the car, lighter in build than his stockier companion, turned in Tishrab's direction, enough to give him a full view of the moving figure's face. He gasped.

*Then a text came into Mazil's phone. He looked incredulous when he read it. He said: "Tishrab's not happy. I'm going to take a look," and went out. At that point the Cyclops started to look nervous and glanced at the clock on the wall.*

"Explain," Mazil commanded as he joined Tishrab outside.

Tishrab pointed to the man. "There is he is."

Mazil shook his head. "That's not McCullboy. Why would you think it was?" He paused, then laughed drily. "Would I be right," he ventured, "in thinking that you spoke to that man on Monday, under the impression that he was Mr McCullboy?"

The earth failing to oblige by swallowing him up, Tishrab could only nod assent.

"That might explain why you got so little sense of out him, mightn't it?"

Tishrab nodded again.

"Idiot." Mazil went back inside. Tishrab saw that the two travellers were aware they had attracted attention, and were preparing to react to any approach.

*When Mazil came back in, he said to the Khan: "It seems we have a McCullboy impersonator outside." This obviously made no sense to him, so Mazil said: "The man that Tishrab spoke to on Monday was not McCullboy, but he is here, now." The Cyclops was getting more and more agitated and kept looking at the clock. Nikos and I both noticed this, and we said so. The Khan pulled a gun and made the Cyclops stand against the wall. Mazil frisked him and said: "He's clean." The Khan told Mazil to keep him covered, then put his own gun back in his pocket. He pulled the storage device out of the laptop and handed it to me. "Just in case," he said. I put it in my bag, then the Khan went out to see for himself what was going on. Nikos and I went after him. I suppose we both guessed that they were onto Peter and Konon, and if so, we might be able to stop things from getting any uglier, although we were still bothered by the way the Cyclops had been reacting. In any case, if the Khan felt safe outside, we might be safer there, too, than in a small room with a man holding a loaded pistol. So we went.*

Tishrab winced as the Khan came out, but the Chief ignored him and went up to the two travellers. "Can I help you, gentlemen?"

"I don't know," said the more heavily built of the pair. "Are you the owner of these premises?"

The Khan gestured expansively around him. "All this is my constituency." He turned to the other stranger. "I understand that you impersonated Mr McCullboy when my assistant spoke to you on Monday. Why was that?"

"*Impersonated* is putting it too strongly," said the erstwhile double. "There was a mistake, it was a delicate situation, and I didn't feel obliged to enlighten my interlocutor."

"Who, exactly, are you, and what is your business here?"

It was the girl from the newspaper who answered the Chief's question. "They're friends. We're brought them as backup."

*The Khan was annoyed. He said: "You might have told us." But that seemed to be the end of the matter and he looked ready to go back into the building.*

A van came up the road from Erimopolis. It slowed a little by the window of the back room, then sped into the forecourt, a charging frenzy of metal and wheels. Tishrab leaped out of its path and dived behind the standing pile of tyres. Ferood vanished.

*We were all on the ground, except Nikos, who was still on his feet because he stayed where he was to push me out of the way. Then it hit him.*

Tishrab kept his hiding-place until the cessation of the shooting that he heard on the forecourt. The shooting started after the van stopped and its back doors opened. Two Haman guerrillas leaped out, rifles ready. But the Khan and the two strangers were by then back on their feet and firing. The guerillas fell before they could get off a single shot. The defenders were reinforced by Mazil, who had left his post in the back room where he had been guarding the Cyclops. Since the Cyclops himself had dropped to the floor on hearing the crash, Mazil had concluded that his own presence was more urgently needed outside than within. He reached the forecourt in time to see the van spin around to make another pass at the party on foot. The driver's front-seat companion had lowered his window and was taking aim. Mazil shot at him. Hit. Meanwhile, the Khan and the strangers made sleet of the van's windscreen, sending the driver slumping down and the vehicle lurching on across the road until it snagged on the rude slope, its career broken.

*I finally dared to get up to half-height. Konon was leaning over Nikos. He shook his head. Then I threw up. Sorry.*

Tishrab poked his nose over the tyres like a Chad. Three fallen men lay in the forecourt. The Sardonikan, whom Tishrab later knew to be Konon Konstantinou, was bending over the body of the photographer and facing the girl. She was being helped by Peter (in Tishrab's eyes, the fake McCullboy) to rise from the ground where she had vomited. The Khan was glancing wildly about.

"Where's Ferood?" he roared. "And that bastard Cyclops!"

"Cyclops is inside," Mazil panted.

"Shoot him!"

"He was on the floor, and still clean."

Venturing a little forward, his hands shaking at his sides, Tishrab could see around the corner, and noticed that the window of the back room was opening. The Cyclops hurled himself through the space: out, down, and up. The Khan fired at him, and he was down again.

"Where's Ferood?" the Khan yelled a second time.

Mazil tried to restrain him. "Ferood might not be in on it!"

"*Might not be!* That clock-watching Cyclops damn well was. Don't you see what happened? If it hadn't been for that halfwit Tishrab and these two clowns, *that* squad would have shot us through *that* window as we sat in *that* room, right there!"

Tishrab was aghast. "Why?"

"*Why?*" the Khan mocked. "Cash flows from Ghimir to the Haman like sewage to plant. The Fund for Rustim Autonomy, gentlemen – " (he addressed his wider audience) " – doesn't get so much as an obol from the Sardonikan State Lottery. *Why?* he asks! I was outbid! Not that I didn't pay the damned Cyclops ten times more than enough for a no-hope hillside haggler turned greasable volunteer! Now where is Ferood?"

Tishrab smelled his own fear and would gladly have used the convenience on the forecourt. But he suspected that Ferood was hiding in it, and he dared not risk delivering him to the wrath of the Khan. The Chief's fury left him perplexed. The Cyclops had betrayed them all, that was clear. He had deserved shooting, and the Khan, perhaps, praise for cutting down a treacherous enemy on the loose. But the man had been running, and was probably still unarmed. Was the Chief, perhaps, no more than a thug, a gangster without honour, without lustre, with no claim to be followed into death's back yard?

Tishrab looked again at the journalist, who had fixed him so searchingly with her clear gaze in the Editor's office, now running trembling hands over blood-drained cheeks, trying to wipe her soiled mouth. Konstantinou put a steady hand on her shoulder.

"Do you have what you came for?" he asked. She nodded, pointing to her bag. "Good girl." He turned to Peter, handing him his own car key, which he had retrieved from the ignition, where Ferood had left it. "Take the lady, take this, take the car and go straight to the Court of Inspection."

Peter hesitated. "What about you?"

"I'll stay and call the cavalry. You go *now* before anyone else turns up. Go!"

On his own territory, Konstantinou was the natural superior. Peter gave way.

*So we took Konon's car. Peter drove. We headed back to the capital.*

The Khan had by then repossessed himself, and, murmuring thanks, extended his hand to Konstantinou. The latter did not take it, but observed: "Sometimes it's the clowns that save the play."

"You've sacrificed your wheels," the Khan acknowledged. "Want to come with us?"

Konstantinou shook his head. "There are six men down. One was ours. I'll stay until the gentlemen arrive."

"Be careful," the Khan counselled. "Ferood is still unaccounted for." He gestured to the Land Rover. "Tishrab! Drive."

Certain that a mere look, silently entreating to be left alone, would win him no pity, Tishrab raised his hands, so that it was plain to the Khan and to all that their shaking rendered them quite unfit for wheel and gear stick.

Mazil intervened. "Give me the key." Meanwhile, Konstantinou was making a call.

"Ferood's Garage on the Erimopolis road. There's been an attack with a vehicle and firearms. Six dead, and a crashed van. Sorry? There is? Well and good. I'll wait." He turned to the departing Autonomists. "Someone's already called the emergency services. The Army, no less, is responding and is on its way."

"Ferood," Mazil surmised. Khasra Khan spat on the corpse-littered forecourt.

"Well, what do you know?" Konstantinou grinned. "Ferood might be innocent after all."

As the Land Rover moved out of the forecourt, circling towards the hills, Tishrab (in a back seat) took a last look through the rear window. He saw the toilet door opening and Ferood emerging, hands held high as Konstantinou, still correctly cautious, covered him with his gun.

*And what more do you know?* thought Tishrab. *I was right!*

# IV.2. Mr Secretary

General Leonidis was in his office at Inner Command when Major Ravdos came to him with the news that Konon Konstantinou was at Shield Base in the Disputed Zone.

The General sat up sharply. The base, said the Major, had been alerted after a call to the emergency services following a Haman guerilla attack at a garage near Erimopolis. A newspaperman, it seemed, had been run over and killed by a squad attempting to assassinate Khasra Khan. The Khan had been there with two of his staff and a pair of journalists, who had in turn engaged Konstantinou and a colleague as backup. The hit had gone wrong; all the guerillas were dead, along with a Rustim militiaman suspected of being their agent. By the time the helicopter had arrived, five of the survivors had already gone, leaving an armed Konstantinou, a mortified mechanic, a stranded vehicle and six corpses.

*Déjà vu, déjà entendu:* the General's worst memories echoed as he listened. The first shock of the news that the mine-clearance team had been all but wiped out. The cold faces of his eight dead men taken up from the ridge. His meeting with the returning phantoms, Konon Konstantinou and the Englishman, Peter Lotsmore. The chill conversation with his superior, forbidding him to proceed with an enquiry. The curt, bitter explanation that the Department had taken matters out of his hands. As he cast his eyes across the desk in front of him, the General was momentarily distracted by the framed image of Nia, sitting on one side of a smiling Athanasia and trying to pull the hair of Kosmas on the other side. Then memory again stirred up the face of Konon Konstantinou and the harsh tale that Major Ravdos had just told.

The telephone rang. Sitting up stiffly in his chair, the General picked it up, to learn that the Secretary of State for Defence was on the line for him.

"General," Mr Secretary began, "are you aware of what's happened near Erimopolis?"

"I've just been informed."

"Well, General," Defence continued, taking his breath at the beginning and holding it as he plunged, "this is of course an incursion of the Haman into Rustim lands which is of course extremely serious and represents an aggression on the part of the Haman which of course necessitates an immediate response namely the creation of a twenty-kilometre exclusion area south of the existing *de facto* limits of Haman territory, do I make myself understood?"

The General scarcely had time to take in the enormity of the proposition. "Pardon me, Mr Secretary, but do I understand correctly that you want to me to go in to set up an exclusion area immediately?"

"It's exactly that, I'm afraid, General. When I say 'immediately,' I mean of course that we want those positions to be secured in the next thirty-six hours. Oh and another thing – "

"Yes, Mr Secretary?"

"Remember that the revised legal framework for security in the Disputed Zone is now in force. The President has just signed an executive order that puts the whole of the Zone under martial law. No party to this morning's carve-up is allowed to leave the Zone without a permit from this Department. Your man Konstantinou and the idiot garage owner are now officially detained by the military police. The Khan and company have bolted: find them and put them under arrest. Do I make myself clear?"

"Mr Secretary – "

"Thank you for the confirmation, General. Counting on your readiness, as always, General. Goodbye," Defence said lightly in conclusion, and hung up.

General Leonidis stared in dismay at Major Ravdos. The latter raised his eyebrows a fraction and asked mildly: "Everything under control, sir?"

The General continued to stare at him, or rather past him, as if appealing from the present moment to a higher tribunal competent to judge it. "They want us to set up an exclusion area between Rustim and Haman territory, pushing the Haman twenty kilometres south, positions to be secured within thirty-six hours."

"In other words, sir, it's the immediate re-creation of the last government's buffer," the Major observed.

"It's exactly that," the General responded, quasi-liturgically.

"Which we have been told was an impractical, undesirable and unrepeatable measure, up to and including this week's statements on the question, sir."

General Leonidis let his fist fall hard onto the desk in front of him, then frowned at his momentary lapse of temper. The blow had not been especially violent, but he was vexed by this fleeting indulgence of the demon tantrum. He glanced at the divine serenity of the Christos Pantokrator on the wall, then back at the waiting Major, whose silent presence expected further instructions. The General sighed and lowered his head. Konon Konstantinou was once more a harbinger of mayhem, death and bizarre reactions from the Government, only this time a cruel circle seemed to be closing. The events of six years ago had been followed by withdrawal from the buffer strip. But now the General had to occupy that same territory, precipitating, in many ways, a return to start. At the same time, too many new factors were jostling. The General sat for a while, pondering what was at stake.

"I want all staff notified at once," he said at length. "And get a helicopter ready. Tell Shield Base I'm on my way to see them. I want to talk to Konstantinou."

# IV.3. The Servant of God

When Ralph was halfway to the Department for the Interior, he was surprised to see a large saloon car pull up assertively in the middle of the road, just ahead of him. A rear window descended, revealing the bearded head of a back-seat passenger smiling broadly at him. It was Father Grigorios, offering him a lift to the Department.

Ralph was suspicious at the sudden consideration from one who so far that week had not favoured him with more than the gruffest courtesy. Having no reason to refuse, however, he got into the back next to Grigorios, and the car moved off into the circulation of the city. Ralph looked up as soon as he was seated, and met the eye of the front-seat passenger, who was turning to fasten him down with his rapier gaze. Ralph was startled. He knew at once that he should have expected the august passenger, but somehow he had not. It was Archbishop Theodoulos, a shade more shrunken after ten years, but with no loss of hieratic *imperium*.

Beams of triumph danced in the old man's dark eyes as he peered at Ralph over the back of the front seat. Ralph found himself taken completely off his guard. The Archbishop continued to pin him down with his gaze. The driver of the car, whom he recognized as the friendly Father Papias, glanced back with smarting embarrassment.

"Monsignor," Theodoulos began, "what can I say? Better still, what can *you* say? That is, perhaps you could tell us what your strategy is meant to achieve, and why it is such an improvement on ours?"

The gleam of vindication shone again in the old man's eyes as he silently defied Ralph to reply. Ralph thought quickly, finding he had been granted a space to draw, but perhaps only to be cut when he made his move. He said mildly: "I'm sorry, Your Beatitude, if you're not satisfied with the ways things are moving. Pardon me if there's some factor of which I'm unaware, but it did seem to me on Tuesday that to challenge the Government to remove Article 6 was the obvious way to throw them off course."

Grigorios intervened. "Really? We were doing perfectly well without it. It was a total impasse, which was fine by us. Your little diversion proved to be somewhat double-edged, wouldn't you say so?"

"Maybe so, but I had the impression that you were glad of it at the time," Ralph observed. "Besides, you saw through their manoeuvre yesterday, didn't you? I would say that you've gained time, and lost nothing."

For a moment Grigorios was checked. Then he retorted: "This cavalier attitude, Monsignor, is exactly what you showed on Tuesday when you dismissed the importance of Article 2." He sounded genuinely disappointed, as if he had expected better of the Ralph Longhand he remembered from happier times.

"Article 2 is a distraction," Ralph insisted. "It doesn't take away the status of the Orthodox Church. The Constitution protects that. The article only foresees an analogous juridical approach to other religious bodies."

"A distraction," Grigorios echoed. "But convenient for the Pope if he were ever to think of setting up a hierarchy here."

Thinking it better not to set foot on that ground, Ralph pressed a different question. "Are you sure you're not underestimating your opponent? Surely she's waiting for the moment to do some kind of deal with Erithia and Eftropos that would split the Holy Synod?"

Ralph had addressed Grigorios, more bluntly than he would have spoken to the Archbishop, but it was the old man himself who replied. "No doubt, Monsignor," Theodoulos began, "you have been given to understand that that those two venerable sees are the weak points in our armour, and that our enemy would seek to undo us at those points?"

Ralph granted that it was so.

"And have you seen any evidence," Theodoulos continued, "that those two sees, venerable as they are, are in any way seditious or slipping from our hand?"

Ralph had to admit that he had not.

"Then, perhaps, Monsignor, the situation is not quite as out of control as you may have thought," Theodoulos concluded, with a disarming smile. "And here we come to the point," he went on. "By all means keep your eyes and ears working, twenty-four hours a day if you like; take all the notes you want, make a full report to Nuncio, Cardinal and Pope, but please, don't try to play our hand for us. Do we have an understanding?"

Ralph gazed out of the car window in silent exasperation. He felt like using some very undiplomatic (not to say unecclesiastical) language, but he held his tongue.

As he looked out, he saw the Department building rise up before him. The car had entered the square and was pulling up a short distance from the police checkpoint near the main entrance. Ralph looked back at the Archbishop, expecting that he would have a last word to say before depositing his new passenger.

Theodoulos did not disappoint him. "Saints, Monsignor," said the old man. "It is saints that the Church needs. Not functionaries, special envoys or sacred pen-pushers."

Ralph smiled. "I hope it's not written anywhere that no one can be both."

Theodoulos frowned. "You're too clever for your own good, Monsignor. Unfortunately, you're probably clever enough to get away with it." The car had stopped and Grigorios was already opening the door on his side. "We're here," Theodoulos observed, as if surprised by the fact.

"Yes, Your Beatitude," Ralph replied politely. "Thank you for the lift. If you'll excuse me." He started to ease himself out of the car.

"Monsignor!" Theodoulos called out. Arrested by the commanding voice, Ralph turned, to be met and held again by the sharp eye.

"I know that you know," said the old man triumphantly.

"That I know what, Your Beatitude?"

"*He who sleeps, let him wake up*. That has proved true once again, has it not?"

But Ralph, too, was a professional. He returned a straight regard which (he hoped) gave nothing away, then bowed his head in a pronounced, but not exaggerated, reverence. Then he left the car. Father Papias, in the driver's seat, shot Ralph a last embarrassed glance before turning the car around. As the vehicle headed off the way it had come, Ralph and Grigorios presented themselves at the checkpoint and were admitted to the Department building. Grigorios reached the door first, but stopped and insisted on giving way to the Roman negotiator.

"After you," he said attentively. Feeling most ill at ease, Ralph nodded slightly, and stepped forward into the impersonal traffic of the Department.

# IV.4. Inspector and Prosecutor

As the morning grew tired, when it was too early to go for lunch but too late to have much relish for the task in hand, a receptionist at the Court of Inspection had been beating his fingers mechanically on the keypad in front of him and staring hypnotically at his monitor when two unusual callers appeared before him.

The Court was housed on the east bank of the river, in a complex which contained Chambers, the Prosecutor's Office and the Inspectorate. The whole structure was subserved by a workaday bureaucracy, which (conveniently for the Government) had beavered much and badgered little since its inception. Complaints against the Government were received at the Inspectorate and, if serious, referred to the Prosecutor's Office. If the Prosecutor saw fit, they went back to the Inspectorate for investigation, after which they returned again to the Prosecutor, who was empowered to send them, at his sole discretion, for adjudication by the Court. The great majority of complaints, mostly from members of the public living in obscure parts of the country, never got beyond the initial letter-opener or e-mail reader, as provided for by an effective office discipline which ensured that neither Inspector nor Prosecutor was overworked. So it was that the Court of Inspection had proved to be a domestic Cerberus which, in theory, could inflict a mortal bite on the Government, but which, in the first ten years of its existence, had scarcely barked.

*Until now*, thought the young, bristling Inspector General, as he related to the Prosecutor what had occurred that morning.

One of the strange pair presenting themselves at reception was a man dressed for the outdoors; he spoke Sardonikan Greek well enough, but with a perceptible British accent. With him was a local girl who looked far from disreputable, but whose pallid face and dusty clothes told that she had not spent the last few hours as a civilized person would wish. *A couple of cranks*, thought the receptionist, as he went on with his pad-tapping.

"I've come about a violation of Paragraph 13," the man said softly. The receptionist didn't look up again.

"Thank you, sir, madam," he said, while continuing to strike his keypad. "Please complete an on-line form on one of the monitors just inside the lobby, thank you very much."

The man tried again. "Did you understand what I said? I said we've come about a violation of Paragraph 13 of the penal code."

The receptionist continued to tap, then (as if to prove that compulsory education wasn't entirely a waste of public money) the penny dropped. He broke out into a fearful sweat. For once, there was serious (and urgent) work to do. He picked up his desk telephone and, exhorting the new arrivals to take a seat, keyed in the Inspector's extension. "Could you come down to reception, please? I've got a reported contravention of Paragraph 13."

When the Inspector General arrived, the place was in a commotion. The girl had got up from her seat and attempted to cross the floor in order to get a coffee from the machine. She had collapsed halfway and was now surrounded by a buzz of well-meaners trying to revive her. The man who had come in with her turned to the Inspector General.

"The lady should see a doctor," he insisted.

The man had the same effect on the Inspector General as he had had on the receptionist. He was an outlandish apparition, but he insinuated the gravity of his business with disconcerting conviction. After a moment's reflection, the Inspector General did as he was asked and had a doctor called out. Then he took the man to his office and proceeded to get the bottom (or as near to it as he could fathom) of the strange disturbance. Meanwhile, the doctor found the girl to be unhurt. She needed rest, but after the doctor's departure she was kind enough to make a deposition at the Inspectorate.

As for the man who had accompanied her, he identified himself as Peter Lotsmore, formerly of the British Army, having left with the rank of major. He had come to Kratistopolis, he said, to meet Konon Konstantinou. The Inspector General soon understood that he was speaking to the second survivor of the slaughter of Konstantinou's team in the Disputed Zone six years earlier. His interest gathered momentum as he listened to the strange new tale of treachery and death, right up to its tangible conclusion: the delivery of the storage device, kept safe in the young lady's bag, that contained a recording of the arms delivery supervised by Drustan McCullboy.

"And that's when I called you," the Inspector General told the Prosecutor, "so you could come and see it for yourself."

*Has it all been for this moment?* the Prosecutor asked himself. After graduating from law school, he had practised as an attorney, competent but with a relatively low profile, for nearly fifteen years before joining the legal team of the short-lived Reform Coalition. The victory of the second coalition, dominated though it was by the Social Governance Party, had done his career no harm. Although the Cabinet detested him, he had been appointed to the Public Prosecutor's Office, dealing with cases of electoral law and appeals against local government. In the first year of the subsequent presidency (a more congenial political order), he was made Prosecutor to the Supreme Tribunal for Constitutional Affairs, the highest juridical structure in Sardoniki at that time. From there it was a short but angrily contested step to the same position at the Court of Inspection, the judicial agency of investigation and prosecution mandated by the constitutional reforms of the following year.

The proposed legal framework for the creation of the Court had envisaged the appointment of judges by a cross-party parliamentary commission. The Opposition (*videlicet* the Social Governance Party, *videlicet* the Department of Constitutional Law at Kratistopolis University, *videlicet* Vasilissa Athemistou) attempted to block the whole project. When that failed, Vasilissa tried to have the rules changed. She pressed for the introduction of a second, government-appointed commission, with power of veto over any nomination. She also tried to secure a quota of gender parity on the composition of the Court, despite the fact that the number of judges was set at five. In the end, the majority which the Nation State Party then held ensured the passage of the new Court's legal framework. The Prosecutor had been serving as such from the day the Court came into existence, a year after the reformed Constitution was ratified.

By the time the Prosecutor had served for five years, Vasilissa had entered Parliament and had a post in the Social Governance Party's Department for the Interior. It was known that she had tried to oppose his re-appointment by putting pressure on the then-president, but that president, who was trying to seduce the centre right to his cause, had not wanted to pick a fight over the nomination. So the Prosecutor had served for a further five years by the time that Vasilissa herself acceded to the presidency of Sardoniki.

The Prosecutor watched the film. Although it could not, of course, corroborate the whole story, the Inspector General said that the reporter from *Dikaiopolis* also claimed that her Editor had pictures in his office of the gun-runner McCullboy meeting staff from the Defence Department. The Inspector himself was of the opinion that the Government had never been more vulnerable. "Let me go over to the Department," he urged.

The Prosecutor hesitated. "It's good evidence," he acknowledged. "But it's not proof."

"Yes, yes," the Inspector General agreed hastily. "Give me a warrant to investigate, and I'll get the proof. Once I've got the proof, we've got the Government."

"No, we can't go to the Department yet," the Prosecutor insisted. "Not until you have all the other evidence first. I'm sure you don't need reminding, Inspector, that the function of this Court is not to 'get' the Government, but to determine whether this Government is acting illegally. And if she is," he added with emphasis, "then, as you put it, Inspector, the Court will indeed 'get' her. Now go over to the newspaper and get the pictures that are in the Editor's office. Then we'll see."

When the Inspector General returned from the offices of *Dikaiopolis*, his hands were empty, but his mouth was full of the story. He had found Laios Aigagros standing distraught in the middle of his ransacked office, whimpering when left alone and screaming foully when accosted. Fortunately, the Inspector General had got some sense out of the Editor's secretary. First, Laios had taken a hysterical phone call from the wife (rather, the widow) of the photographer Nikos Palinouros. Next, his office had been raided by plain-clothes police. The whole file pertaining to the assignment had been removed. That the photographer was dead was confirmed by the man's wife, who had had a visit from the police. Of Maria Kalimithea, the journalist on the story, the secretary had no news.

Laios was helplessly unstrung. Aspasia, the secretary, was considering calling a doctor to give him a sedative. The Inspector General, pitying anyone who attempted to approach the poor monster, assented gravely. His one consolation was that he could assure Aspasia that Miss Kalimithea was alive and unharmed. Then he went back to the Prosecutor with a fiercer sense than ever of being vindicated.

"Short of hanging a banner saying *Guilty* from the top floor of the President's Office, how could they make it clearer? If Laios's pictures weren't evidence against them, they'd never have swooped on him like that. Let me go over to the Defence Department. They've given themselves away."

The Prosecutor sat in silent consideration. The Inspector's analysis was keen and compelling, like his counsel. He thought again. Then he called his secretary and had the warrant prepared. Meanwhile, he mentally revisited the reasons for the decision he was taking.

"If our young friend the Inspector is right," the Prosecutor said to himself, "and if he can put the proof in front of you, it's the end of her. If not, it's the end of him. And of you, too. It may even be the end of all of us here. I don't see her allowing this Court to survive a failed prosecution, unless she leaves the structure in place and staffs it with more pliant personnel. She was one step ahead of your Inspector at the first move. But give him the warrant, and we'll see how he gets on at the Department."

The warrant arrived on the Prosecutor's desk. He signed it at once. Taking it eagerly, the Inspector General bounded off to the Defence Department.

The answer was not long in coming. The Inspector General returned in a mighty fury. He had found the Department offices closed to anyone's access, including his own, on grounds of a military emergency in the Disputed Zone which enforced an extraordinary state of alert in the Department. For the same reason, the Office of the President was also inaccessible.

"Well," said the Prosecutor, "no doubt the military activity is real enough, and the fact that she's proceeding in this way means that the emergency will dominate what happens in that building until further notice. How soon you can make progress depends on how long she can get away with spinning this out."

The Inspector General was scarcely satisfied. "So what shall we do next?"

"What can *you* do, you mean?" the Prosecutor retorted. "Well, you can see to it that the investigation warrant is made public and brought up against her. There are plenty who will consider it their duty to do so, both inside and outside that building. You'll have to trust that the machinery of our democracy will do its work."

"And if doesn't?"

The Prosecutor did not reply. What, indeed, was to be done if Vasilissa maintained her blockade was not a question that either of them liked to think about.

# V. FRIDAY

# V.1. The Proprietor (Again)

This time, Lazaros Ben Ezra was relaxing in his conservatory when Laios Aigagros called on him.

Laios had got up late. His helpless rage had given way to a helpless sadness which threatened to send him into childish tears at the least thought of his misfortunes. The old man, seeing that something was badly wrong with his Editor, rose as quickly as he could and ushered the woeful Laios into his study. He poured out more fortitude; Laios took it eagerly and tried to explain how things had gone awry.

"You remember," he said haltingly, "you remember I came to see you about Vasilissa's crime?"

"Which one?" the old man asked casually as he stroked the tabby, Opsiva, who had in the meantime jumped onto his lap.

"You know, the violation of Paragraph 13."

Lazaros Ben Ezra thought for a moment. "Oh, yes," he concluded, without a great deal of interest. "When did you come to see me?"

"Tuesday," Laios reminded him. "It was Tuesday morning. At ten o'clock. Wasn't it?"

The old man seemed vaguely to recall the conversation. "Didn't I tell you to get on the story?"

Laios nodded repeatedly. "Yes, yes, I did. I did what you said: I sent my top people."

The Proprietor beamed at him. "Excellent! They found what they were looking for?"

Laios screwed up his eyes and nodded again. "Yes, yes, more than they were looking for." His grimace marred the whole of his fleshy face as he floundered into silence. Lazaros Ben Ezra stared at him, frowning.

"So what's wrong?" he asked solicitously.

Laios whined through twisted lips. "The photographer's dead. I had the man's wife on the phone yesterday; she'd been to view the body. It was her husband. He was dead. The Court of Inspection got

117

the recording, but I lost all the pictures. The police got to me first. They raided my office yesterday afternoon. Then the Inspector from the Court comes, but it's too late, the Government's already got the whole file. They raided my files right in front of my staff, and I've got the man's wife on the phone, and he's dead, and the bastards are ripping my office apart right in front of me, and there's nothing I can do!" The fortitude in the glass failed him, and he sobbed helplessly.

Lazaros Ben Ezra sat in silence as Laios blubbered. Opsiva, disturbed, jumped down to take refuge further off. The Proprietor opened his mouth to speak, then closed it again wordless, and laid a pressing hand on the Editor's shoulder.

At length, Mr Ben Ezra moved over to his desk, did some rapid writing, then handed Laios a sealed envelope. "Here," he said softly. "You give this to the man's wife."

Laios nodded, looking up at the Proprietor through streaming eyes. Composing himself as best he could, he rose and left the house.

It had been raining, and shallow puddles clung to the streets and gutter. Laios began to cross the road without looking, and had to leap back to avoid being hit by the car that came unexpectedly around the corner. As he jumped, he dropped the envelope near the puddle at his feet.

Once out of danger, Laios hastily retrieved the fallen object and set about rescuing the contents. He tore apart the soggy envelope and pulled out the paper that lay inside. It was a cheque drawn on the old man's personal account. When Laios's eyes fell on the amount, he gasped and staggered, almost falling again into the path of a passing car.

It was three times what, he, Laios, had earned in the last five years.

# V.2. The Family

Peter woke up in Konon's house and had a shave, feeling inexpressibly better for nature's restorative, not to mention the hot running water and the tender slicing of steel about his chin.

His return to the house had been an ordeal. Maria had insisted on going home. It was all right, she had said: her flatmate would soon be there. So Peter had seen her back to her apartment, then made his solitary way to face Leaina, who had screamed at him the moment he arrived. Although, as he soon learned, Konon's absence was no surprise to her, no one but himself was available to be yelled at, and he had better take it. After all, he reflected, if it was possible (in his own Church, anyway) to marry by proxy, why shouldn't there be such a thing as vicarious marital punishment, at least in extreme circumstances?

Konon had, in fact, called Leaina first from Ferood's Garage to say that there had been "some trouble." He was going to Shield Base to help the military police deal with it. Peter would explain, he had told her (*Thank you, Konon*), since Peter had gone on ahead in the car with one of the journalists, and would, all being well, make his own way back. As if this had not been sufficiently disconcerting, Konon had called again, this time from the base, with the news that he was now, in effect, a prisoner of the Army, or, as he preferred to look at it, of the Defence Department.

Peter had insisted on a large whisky (neat) before discharging his duty of explanation. To be fair to Konon, the matter was indeed better narrated face to face than over the phone, but that meant that Peter was in the newsreader's seat, *nolens volens*. Unlike a newsreader, however, he had been directly exposed to audience response, of which he had already had a preview. He had felt thoroughly spent by the time he had gone to bed.

119

Now, as he came downstairs and headed for the kitchen to make himself some breakfast, he heard excited voices, mostly male, coming from the living room. When he joined them, carrying his rolls and coffee, he found Leaina surrounded by a posse of relatives, gesticulating, comforting, gossiping and commiserating. Some of them came up to him to shake his hand or clap him sympathetically on the shoulder, while others eyed him suspiciously and made no attempt to hide the fact that they were muttering about him.

Peter sat down with his breakfast in front of the television. He was in time to catch a broadcast of the international *Planews Earth*. Garth Browregard looked out from the illuminated screen.

"The British Government's delegate, Lord Bathscombe, is in Paris today for the world summit on a unified policy for Vehicle Emissions Tax. Lord Bathscombe is leading the way in proposing the British VET model, a programme including the new Sustainability Charge levied on all new vehicles. Semele Spooning is in Paris."

Peter watched as the earnest, oval-faced reporter hemmed in the even more earnest British peer. She looked as if she were trying to feed him the microphone, like a solicitous mother with a heaped helping of nutritious rice pudding, hardly to be refused.

"Lord Bathscombe, can you tell us your recipe for an effective VET?"

"Well, we know," the peer began, "that the present levels of private vehicle ownership are unsustainable. That's why, in addition to licence tax, taxes on fuel, and congestion charges in all city centres, we decided to levy a further charge on all new vehicles. That's the Vehicle Emissions Tax. This enables us to have the funds to continue meeting our sustainability targets. A kind of counter-measure for the planet, if you like."

"And will the British programme achieve a corresponding reduction in the costs of public transport?"

Lord Bathscombe didn't flinch. "Well, of course," he replied, "there are things that we'd like to have as targets in each budget, but the reality of determining our priorities means – means that we have to make a choice, and so there are areas in which we would like to do more, but for the moment we are continuing to meet our existing targets."

Back in the studio, Garth Browregard frowned out at the viewer. "And breaking news from Eastern Europe: the Disputed Zone in the southern part of Sardoniki is the scene of renewed conflict. Last night Sardonikan forces intervened to counter an incursion of Haman guerrillas into Rustim territory. The Haman aggression began with an attack yesterday morning in which six people, including a newspaper photographer, are believed to have been killed. More details will be available in our next edition."

Peter's phone rang.

"Peter!"

"Hello, Mum." He slipped into the next room.

"What's going on? Is there fighting over there?"

"Have you been watching television again? I'd turn it off if I were you."

"Is there fighting or not?"

"That's all in the Zone. Don't worry: I'm keeping out of it. I'm safe at Konon's."

"Are you sure you don't want to come back earlier?"

"Oh, I don't think so. I'll be fine here till Monday. Can you guess who else is here? Father Ralph."

"Really? Fancy that. I thought he wasn't stationed there any more. Is he on holiday, too?"

"No, he's working. He's on a special assignment."

"That's nice. Give him our love. Oh, before I forget: the police were here on Monday morning, just after you'd gone to the airport."

"The police? What did they want?"

"You, or so they said. We told them you'd gone to the airport. They said you'd failed to appeared in court after a summons. There must have been a mistake: your Dad noticed that the name on their warrant was *Peter Leastmore*. We tried to tell them, but it didn't seem to sink in. One of them saw your picture, and said: 'Is that your son?' 'Yes,' we said. So off they went. The odd thing was: we saw on the news the next day that they'd arrested someone at the airport later that morning but let him go a couple of hours afterwards. Since we'd not had any bad news from you, we took it they'd got the wrong man yet again."

Peter laughed. Deep, dry, loud laughter.

"What's so funny? The poor man. It *was* almost you, you know. If you'd been there when they called – "

The vexed head of his hostess appeared at the door. "Why are you laughing all of a sudden?"

"Sorry, I'll explain in a moment. – Look, Mum, I'd better go. I'm in demand here. Don't worry about the news. Turn it off. I'm fine here. Really. Yes. Yes. You too. Bye."

Leaina had gone back into the living room. Hearing her voluble altercation with several familial voices, Peter thought he had better take advantage of his respite to call Maria. It also occurred to him that he didn't feel like calling Alice. Maybe he ought to. What if she, too, had seen the news and was alarmed or suspicious? No, he told himself: if she were worried, she would call him, or his folks. And it was not at all certain that she was following the events, anyway. He dared not incur The Displeasure a second time by phoning again inside the no-call period. So the only number he selected on his cell phone was Maria's.

"You all right?" he asked.

"As it goes," the tired voice came back. "Laios has given me the day off."

"I should damn well hope so."

"But Nikos's wife wants to see me later on. Not looking forward to that."

"I can imagine." Peter almost said that it been hard enough trying to keep Leaina calm, but he thought better of it. "Keep me up to date," was all he said.

"You too," she replied. "And Peter?"

"Yes?"

"Thank you. Again."

"Keep me up to date," he repeated, and ended the call.

Returning to the living room, Peter tried to join in the conversation a little, but the hubbub was so rapid that it kept moving beyond his speed. And some of the family were still making no secret of their unfriendliness towards him. He slipped outside and saw an unmarked van, a very recent addition to the neighbourhood's fleet, parked on the other side of the road, opposite the house.

One of the younger men (Leaina's nephew, probably) joined Peter in the doorway. "Something wrong?" he gruffed.

"Something odd," Peter conceded. "That van wasn't on the street until yesterday evening. It's still there. Do you see signs of work going on anywhere?"

The nephew (if such he was) reflected for a moment, then made angrily to leave the house in the direction of the van. Peter intercepted him.

"Don't!" he warned. "Go back inside. Go back and sit down."

Firmly shutting the door behind him, Peter compelled a return to the living room. The young man obeyed but chafed, rambling insolently and throwing bilious remarks out at his audience. Peter turned to Leaina; she met him with a look that was at once plea, challenge, accusation and cry of distress. He took it squarely for as long as he could, then looked away.

# V.3. The Opposition

Ralph arrived at the Department offices, wishing more than ever that he didn't have to.

The previous day had been particularly fruitless and unpleasant. Vassos Varvaros had tried to get them to drop their insistence that the Government contact the International Compliance Commission. The delegates of the Holy Synod had refused to give way, and Ralph had been obliged to support them. Varvaros had become an embodied tantrum. There was every likelihood that today's afternoon session would be more of the same.

When he entered the conference room, Ralph was alarmed by the confident smiles on the faces of Father Grigorios and his team. Such smiles promised victory, but that was hardly to be secured so soon.

Vassos Varvaros opened the proceedings. He seemed to be striving heroically to keep his temper. "Reverend delegates, you requested that the Government contact the Commission over the exclusion of Article 6 from the terms of the referendum. I have one thing to ask in return. If the Government accommodates your request, will you accept the Commission's decision as final?"

Father Grigorios smiled benignly. "Yes, Mr Facilitator. We will."

Ralph was horrified. How could they make such a concession so easily? Of course the Commission would say no, but if the Holy Synod held out against the Commission, he himself could still argue that the Government should exclude Article 6 on its own authority. He could scarcely do that if the Holy Synod agreed to accept the Commission's decision. His attempt to eliminate Article 6 had failed. It would be all or nothing again. Which, he reflected, was exactly what Archbishop Theodoulos and his non-negotiators wanted. The Holy Synod would try to win by persisting with Vote No. Only the remote possibility that No would prevail could save the country from the unmitigated entirety of the Charter.

Grimly, Ralph looked up and saw Varvaros luminous with satisfaction. Mr Facilitator had no doubt read the situation exactly the same way as Ralph himself, and was every bit as delighted about it as Ralph was sick. Varvaros effused thanks and congratulations to all, even managing a cheery nod in Ralph's direction, and adjourned the session.

The delegates rose promptly and made for the door together. Ralph pursued them and caught up with them on the stairs. "I don't quite understand," he said, measuring his words. "Wasn't it worth trying to get them to knock out Article 6?"

Father Grigorios laughed jovially. "Aren't you glad to be out of that conference room, Monsignor?" he retorted. "Don't worry. The Government will never get around to asking the Commission. The Government is about to fall. We're off to watch it happen. Want to come with us?"

Without a word, Ralph followed them across the courtyard to Parliament. Once inside the building, the five delegates of the Holy Synod walked into the lift that would take them to the Chamber. As Ralph was about to step in after them, a voice behind him called excitedly: "Monsignor!"

He turned to see Ektor Pampragmon hurrying towards him. The door of the lift shut, separating him from Grigorios and his team, who were carried up to the Chamber.

"You're just in time to catch the action, too, I see!" said Ektor, pushing the lift's call button.

"Action is what I've been promised," Ralph acknowledged. "But if action is as scarce as explanations, I fear we'll be disappointed."

"Why, don't you know what's going on?" Ektor exclaimed. "There's a cross-party motion of No Confidence in the Government. Nation State's leading it, of course, but the League is backing it, and they've even got one of her own party members as the third sponsor."

"What are the grounds?"

"Well, first the obvious ones," said Ektor. "That she's to blame for what happened on Tuesday by refusing help from the Army, that she's giving WIASCO too free a hand in the Disputed Zone, and now that she's risking war with Ghimir by attacking the Haman. But from what I hear, our friend McCullboy has been caught out. I told you the other day he must have been in town to see the man from the Department. Well, apparently *Dikaiopolis* got hold of pictures of one of their meetings. And the Court of Inspection has a lot more than that."

"Go on," said Ralph, as they stepped into the lift.

"It seems that the Khan, who is unaccountably absent just when you'd think he'd have most to say, offered *Dikaiopolis* the story that the Government's been practising works of mercy among the Rustim militia. Arms-giving, that is. Highly illegal. So much so that the Esteemed Leader of the Rustim Autonomist Party could no longer restrain himself from doing his civic duty in spite of tribal allegiance. So what did he do? He went to *Dikaiopolis* and got them to send a reporter and a photographer with him to the Zone to pick up a recording of an arms delivery allegedly supervised by Mr McCullboy. The Haman got wind of it and sent a squad to take out the Khan. They botched it, but the photographer was killed. The reporter is alive, though, it seems, along with two minders the pair had brought as backup."

Ralph looked at him, aghast. Startled, Ektor understood.

"What's wrong? Do you think it's Maria?"

"It would explain that call on Tuesday, wouldn't it? All the secrecy."

Ektor saw that it would indeed. "But if so," he insisted, "she's alive, as the story goes. And thanks to her, or whoever it is, the Court of Inspection has a recording of the delivery."

Ralph also guessed at the identity of the two minders, but kept it *in petto*. The doors of the lift opened onto the level of the Chamber. Ralph followed Ektor as the latter sprang out towards the Observers' Gallery.

The security guard on duty opened the door which gave them access to the gallery. As Ralph walked in after Ektor, he saw Grigorios and the others looking down eagerly at the Government and the assembled representatives. The leader of the Nation State Party was in mid-narrative.

"The Court of Inspection is now possession of the recording, and has begun a full investigation. There were, I am told, additional photographs of Defence Department staff meeting the British mercenary. The Editor of *Dikaiopolis* had the pictures. But when the Inspector General came there from the Court, yesterday afternoon, he found that the police had already been and gone. There were no more pictures, and no cooperation from the Defence Department, which, burdened by operations in the Disputed Zone, was ill-prepared to grant the access sought by the Inspector. The investigators have found the Office of the President equally indisposed to let them have the cooperation which they had looked for.

"Esteemed Representatives, esteemed colleagues." He paused, looking gravely around the Chamber. "My Party is second to none in the respect and honour it awards our Army in its difficult and dangerous duties in the Disputed Zone. Indeed, we think it cynical of the Government to take occasion from the peril of our troops, and of our citizens, to block all access to these investigations, which legally require compliance. While we commend the conduct of operations by the Army, this intervention raises questions, questions which the Government cannot be allowed to avoid. Is there really no alternative but to continue to push the Haman militia towards the Ghimir border, in circumstances which, ten years ago, brought us to the verge of war with that country? War was at that time averted only by the fall of a government as reckless as corrupt, acting in manifest bad faith. Today, esteemed colleagues, we have, as we had then, such a government. I am confident you will not fail to draw the consequences, or to act on them."

Nation State put his head back and his chin up, roused by his own call to the ballot and defying the event to go otherwise. Ralph watched

Vasilissa as she sat in the President's chair. It was clear that nothing would happen before she replied. She did not hurry. But as the tension began to rise past the tolerable, she rose deliberately, looked straight out across the Chamber, and spoke.

"Is it so? If it is, go out and vote. Go on: pass a vote of No Confidence and force an election. Sit in this chair, one of you. The Esteemed Leader of the Nation State Party, perhaps. After all, why tolerate such an unfit administration when there is a competent alternative waiting to step in?

"For there surely is a ready alternative. The Nation State Party is ready to form a government. Isn't it? In March last year it hesitated, that can't be denied. An election was the very last thing that the Esteemed Party Leader wanted at that moment. But that was eighteen months ago. Confidence has returned. And why not? After all, the last time a government fell from power in a time of military emergency, the Nation State Party assumed control safely and effectively. There is just one small difference between then and now, of course, in that armed conflict was then only a threat. Today we are engaged, and on our own territory. But that is a mere detail. Let us not split hairs. It is, in the end, all in a day's work.

"Perhaps, then, we would do better to stop caviling and explain the whereabouts of the Esteemed Leader of the Rustim Autonomist Party, for whom everyone is now so charitably concerned. After all, when that Esteemed Party Leader is absent from urgent parliamentary business concerning the region for which he is representative, it's obvious that this Government is responsible. Someone might want to say in our defence that if the esteemed gentleman was indeed in the Zone when the emergency arose, there might be any number of impediments to his presence here. But no one, however well-intentioned, should say that on our account, for the absence of the Esteemed Party Leader is quite clearly our fault.

"If it is so, and it surely is, go out and vote. If the Esteemed Leader of the Nation State Party were sitting in this chair, no doubt he would conduct the military operations irreproachably, and at the same time cooperate with any enquiry coming from the Court of Inspection as if the security situation were completely normal. A delicate coordination of military, governmental and international resources is needed to contain the emergency, but the Esteemed Party Leader has more than demonstrated his ability to *maintain* the balance. Above all, his admirable refusal to make political capital out of the most serious security situation this country has faced in the last ten years is proof that he is a statesman, a leader and a gentleman worthy of the admiration in which we hold him. Go out and vote."

In that moment, many eyes met anxiously across the Chamber, but no voice piped, no backside rose from the chair it occupied. At length, several senior members of the Nation State Party began to confer in an urgent undertone with their leader. His eyes moved helplessly to the seats of the Patriotic League. The leader of that party, equally helpless, was receiving the same attention from his own entourage. As for the Government party, at first hardly any dared whisper, look around or rise. Then a few turned to look at the Esteemed Representative who was the third sponsor of the No Confidence motion. All eyes bore down on him. He almost fell out of his seat, lurching across the floor as he attempted a rapid exit from the Chamber. A foot crossed the path of his fleeing heels: he went forward and down, hard, onto the floor. A vindictive roar went up from the representatives. Jeers and balls of screwed-up paper pelted the fallen man as he hauled himself to his feet and stumbled out of the Chamber. The silence tightened its grip again as the assembly became aware of Vasilissa, still silently questioning them all. No one moved. With swift subsidiarity, she supplied for their silence. "The session would appear to be ended, would it not?"

Uproar, but an uproar that was impotent and aimless, erupted as the several groups in the Chamber began to make for the doors, protesting, insisting, defending, blaming, cursing. The President watched for a moment, then turned and walked out of their presence. Up in the Observers' Gallery, Grigorios and his entourage stood speechless. When Grigorios finally turned around, the Roman negotiator was waiting to face him. Ralph found the outcome almost amusing, but steeped in the bitterness of the moment.

"And there you have it," he told them. "You've given the Government an advantage, in expectation of her downfall. Now she's seen off a serious attempt to oust her, and strengthened her position, in one stroke. There is no viable, electable alternative in these circumstances, and no one can deny it now. Over to you. And the best of luck."

Grigorios turned and left the gallery without a word, followed by his disconcerted company. Ralph now reckoned with no issue of his mission save ignominious collapse. Maybe he would finally get the release he often hankered after, although he would rather not have it end quite like this. In contrast to both parties, Ektor Pampragmon was elated.

"What a performance! Did you see how she wiped the floor with them? Now she has a full hand, and there's no card that she can't play."

"Except one," Ralph countered. "The Disputed Zone is the unplayable card, remember? No one's ever won with it, and no one's game has ever survived the attempt. She's seen off her opposition for the moment, but there's no reason to think she can do any better than her predecessors if she tries to make that one work."

Ektor Pampragmon smiled. "What was Monday all about, Monsignor?"

"Yes, I know," said Ralph, "she allowed WIASCO to move in on security in the Zone. But if you think that's going to *solve* the problem –"

"I think it's going to make all the difference," Ektor pronounced. "Yes, it may well push matters to a higher crisis point than before, indeed it probably will, but that way lies the solution, I'll bet. She's going to force the situation to the point where the decisive step can be taken, and when it is taken, the whole region will be the better for it. Say what you like about her, she has the courage to see this through. Yes, I think that Monday was the key to this weekend's action." He stirred from his reflections with an eager, enigmatic air. "Just wait," he said, before resuming his way to the exit. "You'll see!"

# V.4. The Pursuers

Near the approach to a farm in the hills by Erimopolis, but out of sight of the farmhouse, an Army transport waited. A source had reported that a Land Rover matching Khasra Khan's was now in the farm's garage; the number plates were not his, of course, but that need mean no more than a precaution. The farm truck, on the other hand, was out of the garage. So the soldiers sat in the transport close to the road, waiting for the return of the truck.

Meanwhile, the Haman guerrillas resisting the restoration of the buffer strip had been repelled, pursued with fire into their own territory. Continuing the assault, the Sardonikan forces drove the Haman further and further south, then came to a sudden stop. The commander on the ground did not dare move forward again without instructions from higher up. He asked for them. His superior did not dare give instructions without calling General Leonidis at Inner Command. He called him. The General did not dare issue new orders without consulting the President. He called her. The President, triumphant after routing the attempt to force a vote of No Confidence against her Government, was keeping a promise she had made on Wednesday to have a drink with her new secretary in the lounge of her office suite. However, General Leonidis persisted, and eventually found the President in blithe mood at the other end of the line.

"Yes, what is it, General?" she sang nonchalantly.

"We've pushed the Haman as far as the border," the General reported. "There is a Ghimir battalion lined up on the border and the Haman are regrouping around them. If we continue to advance, we can scarcely avoid engaging the Ghimir forces."

There was a brief pause, then the President said: "Have no fear, General. Just advance."

"Madam President," the General persisted, "do you want me to initiate armed conflict with a neighbouring state?"

132

This time the reply came at once. "Don't be concerned about that, General," she repeated. "Advance. Even if it means an engagement with the Ghimir positions. With the revised security framework in place, there is nothing to fear."

General Leonidis said later that he would have refused the order had he concluded that this was just the drink talking. But although there was undoubtedly something a little alcoholic in the President's buoyancy, it was just as certain that she was not drunk. There was too much lucidity, too much calculation in the voice for that. The old dilemma had just given him a glimpse of its horns, but not – yet – enough to justify his grasping them, to turn the head of the beast. In sombre mood, he did as he was told, giving the order to advance.

Over the border, obscured at first by tanks and the regrouping Haman, a Ghimir gunship rose and flew into the Disputed Zone. As it hovered over the Sardonikan ground forces, it was spotted by a vigilant eye in space. The Invigilator, aware of the gunship, awaited transmission of a clearance code. No code came. The satellite sent word to a computer in the WIASCO base in Krastina. The computer sent a Tag missile hurtling after the intruder. On the ground, the Ghimir and the Haman were taken by surprise as the gunship burst brilliantly apart over the dark, bristling border.

Then the air strike began. Planes from the WIASCO base came shrieking over Sardoniki and across the Disputed Zone, their transmitted codes protecting them from the unfailing attention of the Invigilator. The planes began to bomb the Ghimir ground forces, driving them back and scattering them on the road to their capital. And there, in a now-classic manoeuvre, an unmarked helicopter landed on the roof of the presidential palace, where Kalgan was taken and flown in handcuffs from the ruin of his regime.

Far away on the hillside road near Erimopolis, the watchers saw the farm truck returning. Waving the vehicle down, they made the surprised driver disembark. One soldier stayed behind to guard him, while the others climbed into the truck and, under cover of that Epeian contraption, pulled up unsuspected outside the farmhouse. They crashed into the house and hauled Khasra Khan, Mazil and Tishrab from the chairs where they sat intent on the television, watching coverage of the conflict.

And at the end of a pleasant evening, Vasilissa and her secretary finished their drinks and went home.

# VI. SATURDAY

# VI.1. The Source

"I'm sorry," said Father Papias, as he sat in a parlour at the nunciature. "His Beatitude was, well, rather brutal to you on Thursday. It was embarrassing, but what could I do?"

Ralph waved his hand. "That's the least of our concerns. Your side has given the Government a free hand, just when 'this Government' is stronger than ever."

"Stronger than ever? That may have been true yesterday." Before Ralph had time to ask his meaning, Papias continued: "I'm sorry I can't stay very long, but I do want you to know that it wasn't me who told His Beatitude your secret. I didn't know it myself until I heard it from him."

Ralph smiled. "Don't worry: you weren't my first suspect. But tell me: what really is going on with Erithia and Eftropos? I had to admit that, for once in their history, they're not acting like loose cannon. Why are they so well behaved all of a sudden?"

"They've never been this frightened before," said Papias. "Theodoulos is sick. You may have noticed how much frailer he's looking. He doesn't have long to live, and they're all terrified that Grigorios will be the next Archbishop of Kratistopolis. Need I say more?"

"Hardly."

Father Papias went on anyway. "Suppose Erithia tried some manoeuvring of its own. Even if it got the right result, Grigorios would see only disloyalty and he would never forget it."

"One other thing," said Ralph. "A moment ago you spoke as though the Government were in trouble. What makes you think so?"

"Well, now that the Disputed Zone has effectively been handed over to WIASCO, the Patriotic League are coming out again to protest."

"Of course. But that's hardly a stir – unless, of course, the ladies and gentlemen of Militprol are taking to the streets again for a rematch."

"That's exactly what they are doing," said Papias. "And that's why I can't stay long. I must get back to the Cathedral before the fighting reaches it."

Ralph understood. "And since the crowd control police don't keep a great deal of control, and with the Army busy in the field – "

"An Army that's not welcome to help on the streets, in any case."

"But what if she really does lose control of the capital?" Ralph wondered. "Surely she'd have to call in the Army."

"Unfortunately, *have to* has some stiff competition from *won't*."

"Would the General intervene anyway?"

"Hardly alone," said Papias, "and not all his officers are to be trusted. You'd find some of them in the Symposion, if you were to look. Men who know exactly what the Government – not just this one, but its predecessors, too – has been up to in the Disputed Zone for the last ten years: arming the Rustim, of course. Some probably know who is paying for it, too. So you see why the General has to be careful."

Ralph nodded. "And so must you, if there's really going to be street-fighting on your way home. Don't go just yet. We'll call out a police escort to see you back."

Papias chuckled. "In the light of what you were just saying, Monsignor, is that supposed to inspire me with confidence?"

# VI.2. The Inspector's Callers

The Inspector General arrived at his office expecting a certain kind of telephone call, now that his investigation was a matter of public knowledge. Sure enough, his secretary gave him a summary of the messages she had already taken that morning. One caller had insisted that Vasilissa had all along been colluding with the military to hide the fact that there were really no survivors of the mine-clearance team that had perished six years previously. The British officer was supposed to be alive, but who had ever seen or heard of him since the disaster? And whoever it was that the military police had in custody, it was certainly not Konon Konstantinou. The caller said that the fingerprints and iris scan of the real Konstantinou should be compared with those of the man who had been claiming to be him for the last six years, and then the fraud would be exposed once and for all. Meanwhile, the Defence Department staff member who had typed up Vasilissa's fabricated interview with Konstantinou and the Englishman knew the true identity of the impostor. The functionary should be subpoenaed at once before the security services caught up with him.

The Inspector General sighed. If only the "fake" Konon Konstantinou were available for the Court to take his fingerprints. For that matter, an interview with the Esteemed Leader of the Rustim Autonomist Party would also, no doubt, be instructive, but rumour had it that the Khan, too, was now a guest of the military police. "Carry on screening the calls," the Inspector told his secretary, and went back to his desk.

One can imagine, then, the secretary's hesitation when, some twenty minutes later, she telephoned the prickly Inspector to tell him that someone was on the line for him with information about the President.

"This one *might* just be loopy as well, but she says she knows the President professionally and that she has precise information about the file that you'll need to locate when you get access to the President's Office. I thought you wouldn't want to miss it, just in case she's genuine," the secretary concluded, a little apologetically.

The Inspector took the call. Afterwards, he described it to the Prosecutor, when they met that morning. "The caller said: *When you finally get into the Government offices, don't just search the Defence Department. Go to the President's own files and take everything on her ex-husband.* She also said that there's any number of people who can tell you that they've seen the British gun-runner meeting the Defence Secretary. But not so many know just how deep Felix is in all this. *Go through the file on Felix,* she said. *That'll put you in the picture.*"

"The lady never gave her name, I suppose?"

"She would say only that she was professionally acquainted with both Mr and the ex-Mrs Saturnian. An ex-employee with a grudge, I guess, but given half a chance I shall certainly go digging where she's pointing."

"And I suspect you would find," said the Prosecutor, "that Felix knows a thing or two about payments coming into the accounts of Mr McCullboy's company, don't you?" He frowned. "If only we could even get past reception in that damned building. For the moment, nothing's moving, and the trouble on the streets is only going to take attention further away from our business."

"For the moment. But if it does get out of hand, they can't keep stalling indefinitely. We will get in there, sooner or later, and when we do, I'm going straight to that file."

"Just as you went to those other files at the newspaper on Thursday?" the Prosecutor reminded him. The Inspector General looked past him out of the window towards Parliament, as if willing the precious data to be there when he finally breached the block. The Prosecutor saw to his joyless satisfaction that his porcupinesque colleague had indeed taken the point.

# VI.3. The Evacuees

Anna Kolouthou stepped out of the basement archive, locking it behind her, and into the lift, pressing the up button.

Anna's arm was burdened with a file, and her thoughts with the mounting rumours with which the corridors were a-whisper, tales of the disturbance in the city (and beyond, some were saying). Anna had called her daughter, who was at home in South-East Park, and told her to stay indoors. Her son was at her parents', out of town, where (please God) he should be safe enough. She tried to dismiss as unworthy the preying insinuations that the President had the situation under less than perfect control. But with her children's safety clamouring for assurance, such anxieties were not so easily despised. For the corridors were also whispering that the Opposition was now applying real pressure, much more serious than the stagey gesture with which they had dared – and lost – yesterday's confrontation. Rumour flitted, and assurance was elusive. The lift drew level with its destination, and the sliding doors disclosed Vasilissa's office.

Anna knocked and was admitted. "Is this file you wanted, ma'am?" She proffered the object for the President's inspection. Vasilissa, at her desk, nodded back.

"There's one more I need," said the President, as the file slid between her fingers from the secretary's hand. "I'm afraid it's got *his* name on it."

"His?"

"Felix. Sorry to speak the ill omen! You should find it where this one came from. Under *Saturnian*."

Anna turned and descended once again to the paper underworld, where ghostly minutes awaited the chance touch of the living. A fit place for a virtual encounter with the self-declared shade that had crept down the line midweek.

*Saturnian.* There it was. Remove file, exit, lock up, lift, going up. Again.

It occurred to Anna, not for the first time that afternoon, that the President's behaviour was a little odd. Why couldn't Her Excellency give her one complete list of all the files she needed, instead of sending her repeatedly down to the basement? Anna had, to her discomfort, noticed the heavy-duty shredder that stood plugged in by the President's desk, but it seemed disloyal even to speculate that it was being used in her absence to dispose of anything that the Court of Inspection would be entitled to see. It was, of course, a malicious, politically-motivated proceeding, but even so, would there not be vindication in transparency?

Felix and Vasilissa, an odd couple. Was there truth in *birds of a feather* even on the far side of the divorce court? That, for Anna, was the most disturbing proposition of all.

As she approached Vasilissa's office (again), she heard raised voices: President and Vice-President. She dared not knock.

HE. – and they insist on calling in the Army!

SHE. Who's in charge up there?

HE. Interior.

SHE. Interior does know that what the Opposition wants is entirely out of the question?

HE. To hell with Interior. I came down to tell you myself that you can't keep this up much longer.

SHE. I said *out of the question*!

HE. They'll force a vote, and they will win it. The police can't cope. And in Erithia they're even less well-equipped.

Anna, shocked, grabbed the door handle. The President, within, must have heard the noise, for she summoned her to enter. The Vice-President, as if reading Anna's thought, elaborated: "The centre of Erithia and its main train station are being held against the police. Here in the capital, we're under pressure as far in as the Central Bank."

Anna was appalled. "Then we're surrounded!"

"We *will* be surrounded if they continue to move towards us,'" the Vice-President agreed. "The police can't hold them."

Vasilissa intruded dangerously into the Vice-President's personal space. "Have you considered – " she began, " – have you so much as an inchoate idea how much advantage it will give the Army over us if we call them in?"

"Hardly," he objected, "when it's the only sane response."

"You've changed your tune since Monday."

"It's not exactly the same symphony. In any case, wasn't it you who approved the General's appointment? I'd much rather have had someone else. But you agreed on Leonidis. And he's done well enough in the field. Let him do what needs to be done here; necessity rules."

"I think," said the President, with fierce restraint, "you're underestimating the consequences for us if we bring the General into this city. Martial law in the Zone, mine here."

"And I *know*," said the Vice-President, shaking, "that you're underestimating the consequences if you don't do it. Your police force has failed. Admit it!"

Vasilissa lost patience with him. "That's enough." It was time for orders. "Go back up there and tell Interior to hold his ground."

"I'll resign first!" cried the Vice-President, and vanished into the lift.

Anna hardly dared look at Vasilissa. She felt thoroughly wretched, afraid and scandalized by what she had seen and heard.

"You found it, I see," the President remarked, as if the fraught interlude had never played. Anna extended her arm, and the file changed hands. "Thank you, Anna. That's the last one. Could you bring some coffee? The Police Commissioner should be here in a moment."

Off stage again, Anna prepared the coffee. When she returned, she found the President already with her guest.

"You were saying, Commissioner?" Vasilissa prompted him, as Anna handed round refreshment.

"It's not good, I'm afraid, Madam President," he owned. "The city centre is proving tough to retake. We think that mere opportunists have mingled with the militants, so that while our men have been busy with the rioters at strategic points, the looters have been able to work under cover of the rioting, as it were. Houses have been broken into north of the city centre, an indecent assault reported in South-East Park."

Anna, unable to suppress a cry, grasped her phone. Her shaking fingers stabbed at the keypad as she slipped into her own office. "Hello, Kassiopi, are you there, darling? Are you all right? Thank God. Good. OK. Now stay inside until I get back. Yes, yes, that's right. It's still not safe outside, but I'll be back as soon as I can. Just bolt all the doors and stay in. Try and stay out of sight. No, no, I just want you to be extra careful, that's all. It's still not safe outside, but I'll be back soon. Take care and keep safe. Stay in, now. Yes, yes. Lots of love. See you soon."

Wiping her eyes, Anna looked back to see Vasilissa and the Commissioner in urgent exchange.

"What do you need to retake the city centre by nightfall?"

"At least one fifth more manpower than I can send in now."

"What if you redeploy the men you sent to Erithia?"

"That should solve the problem of our city centre, but we would lose control in Erithia completely." The Commissioner hesitated. "Might I suggest – ?"

Vasilissa silenced him at once. "No, Commissioner, you may not!"

There was a knock at the door. At a sign from Vasilissa, Anna opened it to the "eunuch" who stood outside.

"Excuse me, Madam President," said the runner. "A message from the Secretary of State for the Interior: Nation State, the League and a splinter group of Social Governance have a motion for the deployment of troops in the cities, and in the absence of instructions – "

Vasilissa cut him off in wrath. "Send the Vice-President back here at once!" As the messenger began to retreat, the lift opened and the Vice-President himself reappeared, a letter held insultingly between his fingers. "My resignation," he proclaimed.

Vasilissa plucked away the letter and fed it directly into the shredder. She looked the Vice-President in the face, calmly this time. "Just go out to the Villa and get some fresh air," she counselled. "We'll talk about this later."

"If you thought I would take that for an answer, think again," he sneered. "I've left another copy, signed, on my desk. Which, but for that, I have cleared." Turning, he stepped back into the lift without another word.

"Madam President," the waiting messenger ventured, "is there any reply for Mr Secretary?"

Vasilissa smiled at him. "Instructions will come as soon as we have finished consulting with the Commissioner," she said. "Tell him that."

Alone with Anna and the Commissioner, the President, true to her word, addressed the latter. "Now, Commissioner, since you were saying that a security threat has been discovered in this building, requiring its immediate closure, you will kindly order the Esteemed Representatives to evacuate the premises at once."

"Understood, Madam President."

"And have my car, driver and plain-clothes officer ready for immediate departure."

The Commissioner nodded. "And a motorcycle escort, Madam President." He turned to the lift. Vasilissa went over to Anna and put a hand tightly about her arm. "I'm going to the Villa," she said. "But you can leave with us. I'll take you home before I leave the city."

Anna nodded gratefully, and they left the building.

While the clamour of the people's representatives was dispersed by their evacuation from the Chamber, the presidential car quietly took to the road, escorted by two police riders. The eastern routes were largely quiet, most of the disturbance being to the north and to the west. Once they passed a gang fleeing south, away from the fiercest sacking, but what had routed the raiders was not apparent.

At least, it was not apparent until the car turned into the next street, into the roadblock.

# VI.4. Old Acquaintance

Peter was sitting in Konon's living room, watching the news. At the first report of the unrest, he had called Maria, and found that she was on the way to her paper's offices. He had told her to call him if she felt unsafe. At need, he could leave Leaina with her lingering relatives and head off in Konon's car. Maria had thanked him very much, but she didn't expect that it would be any worse than Tuesday.

"And we both needed rescuing then, didn't we?" he had pointed out.

Meanwhile, he was following the coverage on *Planews Earth*.

"In the capital of Sardoniki, violence breaks out on the streets for the second time this week just as conflict with neighbouring Ghimir is resolved," said Garth Browregard. "Last night Convention forces entered Ghimir and took its president into custody. Ghimir forces crossed the border into Sardoniki's Disputed Zone on Friday night when Government troops were acting to contain inter-tribal conflict. The Russian Foreign Minister has called the Convention's engagement with Ghimir forces 'a provocation' and the arrest of President Kalgan 'ostentatious stagecraft.'"

*Of course he has*, thought Peter. The East had been quite content to see Sardoniki fractured by the Disputed Zone and hemmed in by Ghimir, leaving WIASCO thus impeded from moving further south.

The presenter went on. "Tizzy Huff is at the WIASCO base in Krastina talking to Convention spokesman Garrison Duello."

The interviewer was nodding seriously as the WIASCO official spoke. "Yesterday's act of aggression on the part of Ghimir demonstrated what we've been saying for a long time," said Duello, "that Ghimir is – was – the major factor in regional instability in this, in this region, and, fortunately for international security, we were ready for them. Thanks to the cooperation of WIASCO partners here in Krastina and over the border in Sardoniki, we have neutralized the

Kalgan regime. That was the necessary step towards stabilizing the situation in the Disputed Zone."

"Can you comment on reports that President Kalgan was removed from his residence in an unmarked helicopter and is being held at a secret location?"

The reply was merely matter-of-fact. "Kalgan is in the custody of Convention forces at a *secure* location in his own country. Proceedings against him for his illegal incursion into Sardonikan territory are in preparation."

Back in the studio, Browregard continued. "Meanwhile, in the capital of Sardoniki, renewed protests by nationalist demonstrators have led to more violence on the streets. I'm talking to Rod Shooter, who is in Kratistopolis. Rod, what is the situation?"

"Well, Garth, it seems that what started out as a political protest has snowballed – rather, fireballed – into multi-city rioting. There are reports of looting and burning not only here in Kratistopolis, but also in Erithia, the country's second most important city. Behind me you can see the Chamber of Sardoniki's Parliament. I can't stand any closer because even now the building is being evacuated following a security alert. I'm told that the President is already out of danger and that the police are deploying all available manpower to bring the situation under control."

"And how are today's developments affecting the political fortunes of President Athemistou?"

"Well, yesterday the President showed herself more than capable of surviving a challenge to her leadership. An attempt to force a No Confidence vote against her Government collapsed in the late afternoon. Today, her opponents have renewed their criticisms, both over the intervention of WIASCO forces and over the situation on the streets. Now the latest emergency, with the evacuation of the Chamber, means that the political hand-to-hand will certainly continue into the coming week."

Peter's phone rang. It was Maria.

"Are you still offering to come out?"

"Where are you?"

"On the corner from the Central Bank. It's scary on the street outside. A few of us are hiding in the car park on the corner."

"Stay there!"

"There's hardly anywhere else to go."

Peter had already picked up the key to Konon's car and was making his way to the front door. "Sorry," he called to Leaina. "Maria's in trouble. I'm going to see what I can do."

Leaina looked up at him with raw eyes, and nodded. The young man who had crossed Peter the day before hurled abuse at him as he quickly left the house.

The unmarked van was still parked across the street. Peter wondered whether he would be followed as he drove into town. There was indeed a car that held its course behind him, even when police diversions twice forced him out of his way. Preoccupied with that observation, he did not immediately think about what he would actually do if he could reach Maria and the others trapped in the car park. Only when he saw the ascent of smoke over the city did he begin to put his mind to that question. He might drive hard down the street to clear any raiders out the way. That is, if he could get onto the street in the first place. It was unlikely to be as simple as it had seemed on the other end of the phone. But he was, in any case, armed.

Turning a corner, Peter pulled up sharply. The road was closed. This time, however, it was no police diversion. He had come up behind an Army tank that sat obstructing the way, its gun pointing towards the road ahead. He was at the rear of a roadblock, which served not to intercept traffic coming into the city, but to prevent departure from it. The car behind him did not follow him into that road.

Two soldiers crossed the space towards Peter. He raised his hands until they signalled to him to lower the driver's window. Meanwhile, a staff car came past, the way that Peter had come, and halted a short distance behind the tank.

"I'm trying to get to the Central Bank," Peter told the soldiers.

"I'm sorry, sir, the Bank and pretty much everything else is closed," said one of the soldiers. "It's safer inside. Have you just come from your hotel?"

Peter was annoyed at being pigeon-holed as a tourist, but he remained amicable. "It's not the Bank I want. I'm trying to reach a friend who's trapped in a car park nearby. Is there any way I can get there?"

"One moment, please, sir," said the soldier, casting his eyes over his shoulder. Peter followed the soldier's glance and saw a saloon car, flanked by two police motorcycles, coming down the road towards the tank. The car braked and spun around in the direction from which it had come, but a second Army staff car drove into its path and cut it off. Soldiers surrounded the motorcycles, compelling the riders to dismount and give up their weapons. Meanwhile, the passengers of the first staff car had got out and were walking up to the roadblock from behind. One wore the insignia of a general, and was talking to his aide, a major, as he went. Peter recognized him. It was Kallistos Leonidis.

As he walked past, General Leonidis spotted Peter staring in his direction from the parked car. He stopped, looked hard at him a second time and walked over to him.

"There you are!" he exclaimed, beckoning to Peter to get out of the car.

"You, too," said Peter, as he disembarked. "You're Chief of Staff now?"

"Come this way!" said the General. "You're just in time to meet an old friend."

As he followed, Peter saw that four people, two women and two men, had got out of the trapped saloon car. One of the men was evidently the driver. The other was being relieved of a pistol by the soldiers. Of the women, one was standing with her face in her hands, while the other looked up fiercely as the General walked towards her. Peter recognized her, too, and understood.

"Madam President," said the General, "given the emergency, I judged it necessary to enter the capital to bring the situation under control. My men are moving to retake the city centre. I also expect that the railway in Erithia will be freed within the hour. In the meantime, we have secured the Presidential Villa. I see that you are heading in that direction, and under the circumstances I can propose nothing better than that my officers accompany you there. There you will be able to make plans in peace and safety. And, of course, you will have the opportunity – " (he paused) " – of cooperating with the investigators."

Vasilissa drew back her right shoulder and swung her clenched fist straight and hard into the General's face. He kept his balance and his silence as he took the blow.

The other of the two women was visibly struggling against her tears, with scant success. She approached the General. "Please, it's my daughter. She's fifteen, she's at home all on her own, she doesn't even have her brother with her, and I need to get back to her. Please let me go home."

The General nodded. "Of course," he said. "Where do you live?"

"South-East Park."

"That way is clear," he said. He turned to the President's driver and her disarmed guard. "Take this lady home," he ordered. "The President will come with us."

The woman turned tearfully to Vasilissa and flung her arms around her before returning to the President's car with the two men. An exit was cleared for it, back the way it had come. The car took her away, down the newly pacified streets.

When the departing car was out of sight, Peter noticed that Vasilissa had spotted him. She opened her mouth for an exclamation which was then suppressed. She peered at him; he guessed that she had at first taken him for Someone Else, then realized her mistake, still unable to identify him although she thought she knew him after all. He did not speak to her, but only to the Major.

"Sorry, but I'm trying to get to my friend. She's trapped in a car park on the corner from the Central Bank."

The General, hearing this, addressed two of the soldiers. "Go there and take care of it," he ordered. "You stay here," he said to Peter. "I want to talk to you when I've seen to a few things." He gave instructions to two of his aides to take the President to the Villa in the second staff car. As they escorted her to the vehicle, the President looked back, her eyes calling wordless odium upon the General.

"I'll be with you shortly, Madam President," the General called to her before conferring with the Major. "Once the whole of the city centre is secured," he said, "we ought to take the airport. WIASCO forces will still be crossing the country to get into Ghimir and the Disputed Zone. I fear that the chance to gain an extra, highly convenient foothold on our territory will prove just too tempting for them."

Peter was alarmed. Should the airport be occupied by the Army on Saturday evening, his chances of catching his flight home on Monday were somewhat compromised. True, if Konon had not returned by Monday, he would hardly be in a position to pack and go home anyway. But was not that now in the General's hands?

The Major had reservations. "Say we take the airport," he said, "how long can we keep it out of action? Once we start hitting commercial interests, sir, our operation could become unmanageable."

The General was unperturbed. "What matters now is that we have control of the situation, and that we show it. Once we've made that clear, we can be as flexible as others will have to be."

"So," said the Major, "we retake the central station in Erithia, finish the job here in the city centre, then go and take the airport."

"And in the meantime – " the General went on.

"Yes, sir?"

"I'll be with you in a moment," the General promised Peter. He turned back to the Major. "In the meantime, call Shield Base. Tell them to release Konstantinou, with transport home. I don't think we need worry about the permit from the Department. The garage owner goes free, too. The Khan and company can go, but watch them. And after that – "

"Yes, sir?" The Major sounded a little alarmed.

"After that," said the General, "you can take the rest of the week off."

# VII. SUNDAY

# VII.1. The Autonomists Unbound

*Four thousand dinaria for a full tank!* Tishrab, appalled, stared at the display on the petrol pump as he withdrew the nozzle from the side of the Land Rover. It was typical for this sort of wilderness station, where default of competition sapped the inhibitions of upwardly mobile prices. At least it was not himself, Tishrab reflected, for whom the bill told. This was Expenses, but still their first piece of bad luck after quitting the hospitality of the military police.

"I want my vehicle back!" the Khan had insisted, on being told they could go free. Since the Land Rover was still at the farm where they had left it, and since no one would guarantee its delivery until morning, they had spent a further night at Shield Base. When the military policeman had remarked that that was actually the safest choice, the Khan had made an unpleasant conjecture about the man's family background as soon as he was out of the room. Early on Sunday, however, the car was there. By an act of supererogatory courtesy, it had even been refitted with its own number plates that they had stashed away at the farmhouse. When "Tishrab, drive!" had been called again, they were off in the direction of Erimopolis, where the Khan kept his constituency office.

"I presume they're tracking us," Mazil had declared.

"Then find a debugger."

"You could ask Ferood."

The Khan had answered with an obscenity inconducive to the progress of that proposal.

One favour that had not been done for them was to top up the tank. A wink of the warning light had told them that they ought not to risk trying to reach Erimopolis without filling up. So here they were, about to pay through the taxpayer's nose for the liquid exigence.

The Khan entered the shop himself to settle up. Since he was not wont to neglect an opportunity for ingratiation with his constituents,

154

his two subordinates were hardly surprised to see him take the present advantage. They accompanied the Chief into the shop, where a single customer stood perusing a paltry stock of accessories. Behind the counter stood the scarfed proprietress, slight, wrinkled, stooped under the weight of eld. At her rear, a paunchy man loitered between the counter area and the back room of the shop.

The Khan courteously greeted the already present customer, who ignored him. Undeterred, he approached the counter, smiling at the ancient dame.

"Good morning, Granny! It's Number Two. Now what do I owe you?"

A bony hand darted from under the counter, heaving out the object grasped within it. A finger pulled, a shot flared out and a raucous voice squawked "*Traitor!*" Only the fact that Granny was just a little less fast than in her prime saved the Khan's forehead from a puncturing. All dropped to the floor, except the other customer, who continued to mull over the equipment, and the corpulent man at the rear, who promptly clamped the hand of the proprietress. Mazil was first back on his feet, reaching for his gun. With obvious relief, he relaxed his grip once the paunchy man had prised Granny's weapon from hers. Tishrab shared his colleague's sentiments. None of them, not even (he still dared hope) the Khan was so bastardly as to take any satisfaction in shooting an old lady, even one who had tried to put lead in his head. The Khan himself sprang up and out of the shop, followed by Mazil and then (he being the last to rise) by Tishrab, who stood fumbling for the car key as the others strained to leap into the vehicle as soon as it was unlocked. To Tishrab's dismay, the Khan ripped the key from his hand, opened the car and jumped into the driver's seat himself. To be driven by the Khan in high agitation was the last thing Tishrab's stomach needed. As he clambered into the rear, he was thrown roughly back and around as the Land Rover charged out of the station and onto the road.

An anxious thought struck him: a new vulnerability they might have incurred before the law.

"Did we pay for the petrol?"

"Shut up!" The Khan accelerated, and they lurched ahead.

The shortest way to Erimopolis led up a mountain track and through a tunnel before descending to join the straight route to the city. The Khan made the ascent and drove the Land Rover into the dark, steering down the tunnel towards the dull daylight on the other side. True to his habitual caution, he slowed almost to a halt before emerging. Then he stopped dead. An Army helicopter passed in front of them before the rock face, close to their exit.

Mazil counselled that they simply wait until the air patrol had gone, then move forward, but the Khan thought that the risk of being seen and followed was too great. Mazil reminded him that they were almost certainly being tracked anyway. The Chief, however, settled on taking a longer, less obvious route. Turning around in the tunnel, he drove out the way they had come. Tishrab stayed in the back and out of the discussion.

About an hour later than was necessary (if you accepted Mazil's argument), they were on the approach to Erimopolis. A couple of cars were ahead of them, slowing down to a stop. The Khan, doing likewise, sent Tishrab out to ascertain the cause of the halt. He hopped out, looked ahead, slipped back in, and hesitated.

"Well?"

Tishrab winced. "Checkpoint."

The Khan looked in his mirror, then over his shoulder at the car that was even then coming up behind them, preempting another retreat by reverse gear. Still leaning back over his seat, he glanced from Tishrab to Mazil and around again.

"Ideas, anyone?"

# VII.2. Sir Priest and Sir Knight

"From Father Grigorios." After Peter had assisted at Ralph's Mass at the nunciature, the priest was briefly called away by the arrival of a courier. Returning to the parlour, Ralph slapped the consigned envelope down on the table, and went back to preparing tea.

Unlike the slaves in the parable, Konon's relatives had had warning – in the person of Peter – that the master of the house was about to return. Some were glad, and, since it was getting late, took the tidings as leave to go home. A few, led by the curmudgeonly nephew, seemed disinclined to believe it until the householder himself turned up and threw them out. Dismissing Leaina's screams of welcome and reproach (*I'm just a little late, that's all*), Konon had sat down, had a drink and conferred briefly with Peter before they all turned in. In the morning, man and wife were up in grateful mood and off to the Divine Liturgy, where, Peter supposed, it would be hard luck on anyone else wanting a chance to light a candle. Since his hosts were showing such prompt piety when anyone might have conceded them a lie-in, he had reasoned that he himself had little excuse for missing his own appointment with Christ and His priest. So here he was.

Ralph opened the envelope, which indeed bore Grigorios's name and address. The sheet of paper inside was completely blank, however, except for a single, large, black exclamation mark in the middle of it. "*Touché*," Ralph murmured, and laid the sheet aside.

"You actually saw McCullboy, then?" Peter remarked over tea.

"Thus spake Ektor, at any rate. He did look vaguely like you. And I suspect he hasn't gone far. Did you notice how the President of Ghimir was taken? Helicopter swoop on top of the presidential palace. Exactly what happened to Nokandu."

"Who?"

"Former president of Meerkatsmark. Another WIASCO regime change."

Peter laughed. "I doubt that WIASCO was expecting the latest one."

"Regime change isn't quite what we have yet," Ralph observed. "More a regime hiatus. But since there'll probably be an election at the end of it, there's a chance – just a chance – that that will have a better outcome than the last one."

"If not, you'll be back for Round Two."

"If the Holy Synod will have me again," Ralph countered. "Speaking of which, Archbishop Theodoulos knows."

"Knows what?"

"*He who sleeps.*"

Peter was taken aback. "How did he find out?"

"I think someone's been doing some research on both of us," Ralph smiled. "It doesn't matter. Of course, I've been keeping the story to myself."

Peter nodded. "What's next for you?"

"Well, as soon as the airport's open again I'm heading back to Rome. There's no point staying here when there are no negotiations. More precisely, when there's no Government to negotiate with. What about you?"

"Like you, wait for the airport to open," Peter sighed. "If I don't turn up when Alice expects me, you know whose fault it will be."

"When's your flight? Or when ought it to be?"

"Tomorrow afternoon. Close, isn't it? Meanwhile, I have to meet Maria for lunch."

"Lunch is the least she owes you," Ralph agreed. "If you let her pay, that is."

"Chivalry is not dead," Peter smiled. "It's just reeling from being kicked in the – " (he coughed) " – once too often."

"My uncle," Ralph recalled, "was once judge in a nullity case where the husband had brought divorce proceedings after his wife pressed his trousers for him."

"That was churlish. You'd think he'd be glad to have his trousers ironed."

"He was wearing them at the time."

Peter grimaced and glanced at his watch. "Well, now we know what I'll deserve if I'm late."

"Just one thing before you go," said Ralph. "Do you have the General's telephone number?"

"I do, as it happens." Peter reached for his phone. "Do you think he might be able help you?"

"I have, let us say, some intelligence which, in the circumstances, I think he ought to hear. Whether anything else comes of meeting him remains to be seen."

Peter read him the number, then they rose and shook hands. "Best of Britannic."

"*Et cum spiritu tuo*," Ralph smiled. "Until the next time."

Peter left the nunciature and made his way to the restaurant where he was to meet Maria. On his way, he passed Ektor Pampragmon standing in front of a television camera.

"No," Ektor protested, "I don't accept that order has been restored. On the contrary. On Friday night, we embarked upon a well-conceived, successful operation to ensure regional security. Last night was the reverse. This country has been plunged into its gravest crisis in modern history. The continued existence of our democracy at stake. The global community must now manifest its will in no uncertain terms."

Peter paused to hear this much, then went his way.

Maria was already at the restaurant when he arrived (although, to his relief, he was not late). She started to chaff him over the top of her menu.

"So what happened to you yesterday? A fine rescuer you turned out to be."

This was hardly fair. "You got rescued in the end, didn't you?"

"Yes," she conceded, "and by two very good-looking soldiers of the Sardonikan Army."

"So it was better than being rescued by me in any case?"

She laughed. "It certainly beats being rescued by Ektor Pampragmon. Once in a week was quite enough of that."

"I can imagine. I just passed him giving an interview on my way here. Do you know what he was saying?"

"Now I can imagine. I could write the script." She scanned the menu. "What are you having?"

"What do you recommend?"

"I'm starting with water," she said, hopping lightly towards the bathroom. "See you in a minute."

Peter watched her go, and saw her bump into a young man across her path. She laughed and excused herself in rapid Greek that he didn't quite catch. The fellow returned the pleasantry and went his way, as Maria disappeared whither she was going.

Peter winced. A moment ago her presence had lit him up, buoyed him up and absorbed him. Now that she was joking inaccessibly in her own tongue with the other fellow, she suddenly seemed foreign to him, and that thought reminded him how young she was (little over half his age), and how remote was her world from the one that was now his. He was a living ghost, haunting old haunts. A new day would make him disappear. The village, the pub, Alice: all these reached further back and awaited him again. At least, the pub and the village awaited him. Nothing else of memory could be counted on for the future. But his future could not be found here. Could it?

Maria returned. They ordered, they talked, they ate well. She insisted on settling the bill, and he gave in. She grinned, victorious.

"How long are you staying?"

"Who knows? I won't be going anywhere until the airport's open again."

"If you left on schedule, when would you go?"

"Tomorrow afternoon. But that's rather a long shot."

"Well, if I don't see you – "

"Likewise."

"Keep in touch?"

He smiled as he lightly kissed her goodbye. "We'll see what happens," he said.

# VII.3. The President's Visitor

"Thanks for your patience, Monsignor. The President will see you now."

Ralph rose, exhilarated to have reached the threshold, but never more sharply aware of the risk he was taking. He had, in fact, been seen leaving the nunciature by Archbishop Shenanigan, who, with polite curiosity, had asked him where he was going. "Across town," he had answered. "It should be safe enough now." It had indeed been his intention (carried out in the meantime) to cross town, namely in the taxi that he planned to take through and out of the city to the Presidential Villa; better, though, not to mention that destination. It was, after all, easier to ask forgiveness than permission.

"Thank you, General," he replied to the courteous summons. "I suppose I should thank the President, too: she doesn't have to see me at all."

"I'm sure she finds you and your visit quite intriguing," said General Leonidis, leading Ralph towards the lounge. "One thing, Monsignor. The warning you were given. Did it actually come from inside the officer corps?"

"It came from one of Archbishop Theodoulos's clergy."

The General smiled. "It was not entirely news to me. I didn't know how well it was known over there. Thank you anyway." He tapped on the door of the lounge, opened it and spoke to its occupant.

From her armchair, the President answered him. "Why, General, what a beautiful bruise you have!"

"All the better to make my wife jealous with, Madam President. Here is Monsignor Longhand."

"Show him in," said the President. The General ushered Ralph into the lounge and left him there with Vasilissa Athemistou. He thanked her for admitting him, and, at her invitation, took a seat.

"So it's you who's been causing the Department staff such agitation," the President observed.

Ralph smiled. "Mr Varvaros is hardworking."

"Odd, isn't it?" said Vasilissa.

"Madam President?"

"Exactly. *Yes, Madam President. Are you comfortable, Madam President? Madam President, there's someone to see you.* And this from a man who's taken over the country at the point of a gun, put the President under house arrest and thinks he can make me cooperate with the damned investigation. But I'll tell you something," she went on. "If the Court put him up to this, they've overshot the mark. Once this is over, their case will never stand up. It's lost all credibility already."

"Then you're confident that you'll soon be back at your desk?"

"Oh, there's no doubt about it. Our strategic importance is now more than clear. There's no way our Convention partners will stand for any attempt on our democracy in the circumstances." She paused and scrutinized him. "And you, how did you come to be chosen for Mission Intractable? Have you worked here before?"

"Yes, I was Second Secretary at the nunciature. Ten years ago."

"Really? That's when I came back. Did we ever meet?"

"We did, in fact. Once. At a banquet at the US Embassy, as I remember, to mark the Ambassador's wife's one thousandth parking ticket."

"O God. I must have had Felix in tow. Correct?"

"We've established the occasion. I see no need to recall the company."

"Very discreet."

"If I may, in return, ask one indiscreet question?" He took the single raised eyebrow as permission to speak. "In the event that we foresee, that is, when you're back at your desk, do you think that this experience of being under pressure will – will make you see anything differently?"

"Meaning?"

"Perhaps the current pressure might give you another perspective on others who are likewise hard pressed. The Holy Synod of the Sardonikan Orthodox Church, for example."

"Aha! You're letting the mask slip. You were on their side all the time!"

"Madam President," Ralph protested, "I made it clear from the beginning that the Holy See sympathizes with the concerns of the Holy Synod. We would encourage them not to be inflexible on all points. But as for the things that they, and we, consider essential – "

"What would you have me do?"

"To put it colloquially, Madam President, not to push it. Exclude Article 6 from the terms of the referendum. You're a sovereign state. No one from outside can dictate what you put into national legislation. As you say, WIASCO can't overlook your strategic importance. Surely that gives you a little leverage."

Vasilissa smiled. "But perhaps there is no coercion, Monsignor. What if Article 6 is exactly what I want in our legislation?"

"Why? You don't need it, and the Church can't live with it. Their conscience does you no harm, and it has its rights. Can't you let them be?"

"That's precisely where you're wrong, Monsignor," said the President. "The enemies of human rights have no right. That's why, as you put it, I'm going to push it."

Ralph nodded slowly. "I see. If you'll excuse me, Madam President." He rose.

"It's nothing personal, you know that?"

"Madam President," he replied, as he bowed to take his leave, "that was well understood."

A soul one hoof-step away from the abyss, he reflected. Although it was not of his fold, he could see it with a shepherd's eye, yet he must speak to it in the strange accents of the embassy. The parish, even the marriage tribunal, had never seemed more inviting. So what if he did get found out, and the clandestine visit cost him his diplomatic career? They could not, indeed, take from him anything that he would more willingly part withal.

# VII.4. The General at Home

It was already late in the afternoon when General Leonidis returned home. Kosmas, Darios and Nia rushed clamouring about him, weapons at the ready. "Dad! Dad!" Kosmas was shouting. "Everyone's talking about you. What's happening?"

"Oh," his father told him solemnly, "lots of big things have been happening."

"Daddy!" Nia called out, pushing her way to the front. "Daddy, I captured Darios in the battle today and I tortured him until he told me where all his warheads are hidden."

The General shook his head. "Not good, sweetheart," he told her.

Nia pulled a puzzled face. "Why?"

"Because," the General explained, "for one thing, it's immoral."

"What does that mean?"

"That means it's bad," he said. "Next, there's no point in having information unless it's true. Now if you torture him, he'll tell you anything just to make you stop, won't he?" Huge eyes and pricked ears followed every word he said. "And for another thing," he said, leaning forward confidentially, "there's always a limit to what you can get away with."

The door of the next room opened, and Athanasia came through it, carrying Linos. The General had reckoned with a battle, but Athanasia, quite collected, was there to parley. She consigned the infant to Kosmas, and sent the whole quartet into the other room under the panting tutelage of Spyros, the Kokoni.

"So where are we?" she murmured, sitting down opposite her husband.

"In a safe place," he declared. "For the moment."

"For the moment?"

"There's the inevitable WIASCO delegation to deal with, but it won't convene until tomorrow morning. We took the airport yesterday before their forces could move on it, which gives us something of a breathing space."

She nodded slowly. "I think I get it. Our airport needs defending from our allies, so you went in and took it."

"That's right," he smiled. "Meanwhile, the fires are out, this city is quiet, Erithia is quiet, criminals and suspected criminals are in our custody. So are the rioters and looters."

She looked him straight in his splendid black eye. "What's the story with the President?"

*Where to begin?* he thought. When the President, on Friday, had ordered an advance on the Ghimir positions, the possibility of refusal had occurred to him, although he had rejected it for lack of certain justification. The democratic clock was still, at that moment, ticking. But that the clock might crack was by then undeniably in prospect. On Monday, the constitutionally dubious hoodwinking of Parliament; on Tuesday, fighting in the street; on Friday, exchange of fire with the southern neighbour. Finally, reports that Kratistopolis and Erithia were burning, and that the President was defying parliamentary momentum by refusing to call him in, had prompted him to seize the horns.

"When I went from Inner Command to the city," he told Athanasia, "it seemed as likely as not that it was already over for Vasilissa." That was how it had been to all *appearances*; how he would deal with Vasilissa herself had at that stage remained open. "Then I heard that she'd ordered the evacuation of Parliament before it could vote for our intervention, and was fleeing east."

"To her Villa, I suppose."

"Probably."

The tone became brittle. "So why not just let her go?"

It was now for him to return the straight regard. "No. Not at that point. Of course, the President could go to the Villa, by all means, but she would not be going – unescorted." One of them, to his mind, must now eclipse the other. He would so hold his course that Vasilissa would never again be in the ascendant, even if his fire, too, must go out of the strange and tormented constellation in which they had been set.

Athanasia nodded again. "I see. You put the President under house arrest when she was already fleeing."

He offered no contradiction. Her voice began to rise.

"And just what made you think you could sit that out? It's not as if it was even necessary by then."

He made scales of his hands, weighing the air.

"Since when has anyone who's tried that been allowed just to walk away from it?" she persisted. "I mean, they've walked, but they've had to go. We'll have to go, won't we? To leave. Leave – home. You see what you've done? To us. To me. To the children. What were you thinking?"

"Do you really want to know?" he asked. She was taken aback, and, falling silent for a moment, let him speak.

"Over six years," he said quietly. "Too much death. Too little accountability."

"Oh, so this is going to bring those men back, is it? I and my children in exile are going to bring them back. Perfect sense! It makes perfect sense! You bloody idiot! You've taken leave of your senses, you stupid boy who never stopped playing with guns!"

*Waff.* The Kokoni's bark rang starkly from the next room.

"And Spyros, too!" Athanasia, collected no longer, rose suddenly. She paused, seemingly struck by a suspicious thought. "That black eye – who exactly gave you that?"

"It's the mark of my service," he said quietly. Athanasia retreated rapidly to the next room, caught up Linos and was soon hastening up the stairs.

Kosmas, Nia and Darios came apprehensively from their cover. The sound of the youngest child's cries reached their ears, followed by a bitter sob from Athanasia. "Why is Mama crying?'" Darios asked. Spyros also looked quizzically at the General.

"Well," said Leonidis, with a friendly smile, "Daddy locked the Witch in her castle so that she can't get out."

The boy was confused. "But isn't that good?"

"I should say so," said the General. "My men did very well indeed. They're the best. Even better than your men, Nia." Nia chuckled and gripped her action figure with tight loyalty.

Kosmas frowned. He, at least, was not satisified. "So why *is* Mama crying?"

"Because she knows," said the General, with a sigh, "that there's a limit to what even Daddy can get away with."

# VIII. MONDAY

# VIII.1. The Invigilator (Again)

At nine a.m., General Leonidis found himself back in the conference room at the Cabinet Office. Major Ravdos was faithfully at hand. The President's chair was carefully kept empty. The tigress, caged indeed, was not there. This time, the General's peril was eyeing him down in the persons of the WIASCO delegation. Garrison Duello looked business-like but relaxed. From time to time, he even smiled: a not-unpleasant foil to the heavy, unmoving face of the military man at his right. General Hamlin T. Wolfganger had been commander of the WIASCO base in Krastina since it was established, when Kalgan of Ghimir had first struck out to the east. To the left of Garrison Duello sat Lord Bathscombe.

"Of paramount concern, gentlemen," Duello was saying, "is, of course, the continued cooperation of all signatory states in pursuit of regional security. Above all, that means continued access to the Sardoniki–Ghimir border for Convention forces. That, in turn, means passage across the Disputed Zone. Without prejudice, of course, to the safeguarding of democracy in Sardoniki once the current emergency has been stabilized. In which connection, the restoration of Kratistopolis Airport to normal operation is an important concern to many of our signatory states."

General Leonidis returned the moderate but determined tone. "We're delighted to find that the objectives of the Convention are in harmony with ours. However, there are a number of points to be clarified as a preliminary to an accord. First, we seek a guarantee of freedom from all outside interference in the legal proceedings against President Athemistou. The second point concerns Sardonikan sovereignty in the Disputed Zone. For instance, the role of Kratistopolis Airport in Convention forces' access to the Zone must be clarified before the airport can be reopened."

Duello frowned a little, but stayed mild. Lord Bathscombe, however, had begun to stir when the General had mentioned the prosecution of the President.

"You must understand, General, that you are in no position to demand anything!" the peer exclaimed. "You are not the Government of this member state, and only a democratic government will be recognized as such by us. It's only to put an end to your little putsch, not to further it, that we're talking to you at all. You should not even think of putting one toe out of line if you don't want to see a decisive intervention from us. You will not dictate terms to us. You would be wise to cooperate with us to ensure the smooth restoration of democracy, law and governance to this member state, because it will be restored, whether you cooperate or not!"

Garrison Duello resumed his thread. "Of course, General, we respect the fact that the prosecution of President Athemistou is an internal matter to Sardoniki. We are perfectly willing to ensure that due process of law be followed, and to that end, we are ready to work with you to establish a timetable for the restoration of a civilian administration, albeit an interim one. At the same time, we very much hope that our sharing of your concern for due process of law will be reciprocated with the cooperation we expect in the matter of regional security. I trust that is understood."

Lord Bathscombe was stirred up again. "And you will release immediately any other members of the legitimate Government that you may illegally have placed under arrest!"

General Leonidis smiled. "All members of the Cabinet are safe in their homes. Under our protection, of course. But not the former Vice-President. It seems he left the city immediately after resigning."

"General Leonidis," said Duello, "let me assure you there is no question of Convention forces commandeering the airport. The economic consequences of its continued inactivity would make that prohibitive." (The General turned to Major Ravdos and gave him a nod of quiet triumph.) "However," Duello continued, "I must emphasize that it is vital to the interests of regional security to assure continued passage between the Convention base in Krastina and the Sardoniki–Ghimir border. Moreover, we have to consider the threat to our operations posed by Haman guerrillas, as well as the possibility that the Rustim militia will escalate the conflict. From now on, security in the Disputed Zone must be the responsibility of Convention forces. This, as you will recall, is consistent with the revised legal framework for security which President Athemistou notified to Parliament exactly one week ago."

General Leonidis and his aide exchanged apprehensive glances. "Gentlemen," the General began, "I appreciate your readiness to collaborate with us to control the situation in the Disputed Zone. But there are a number of facts which surely have not escaped your notice. First, it was precisely the notification to Parliament of the revised framework that precipitated the events of last week. Next, the security emergency in this city, which left me with no alternative but to intervene, was occasioned by protest, and counter-protest, arising from the very measures you propose to continue. You wish for the political stability of this country and a return to effective civilian government. So do I, but unless we, the Sardonikan Army, maintain responsibility for the Disputed Zone, I find it hard to see how that objective can ever be achieved."

Lord Bathscombe guffawed at the General's discomfort. "Perhaps the General has overestimated his own ability to 'restore order'?" he coughed. Garrison Duello smiled again, conciliatory and confident.

"Of course, General," he replied, "the collaborative nature of the framework means that we fully expect to involve Sardonikan forces in the maintenance of security in the Zone. But I'm afraid it's out of the question that we replace the arrangements that are now operative. And, if I may remind you, we have the means to ensure compliance, thanks to our control of passage by air over the Zone. You will recall our presentation, here in this room, of the DZ-1-13 system, also known as the Invigilator. I trust you've become familiar with it in the meantime."

General Leonidis had scarcely had time to register the point when he was surprised by the sudden utterance of General Wolfganger. The WIASCO General was looking across the table at him, saying: "As of ten o'clock this morning you'd better not send anything flying over that Zone, because as of ten o'clock all security codes recognized by our base computer are going to change. So if you want to fly anything in that airspace, you have to talk to us. Otherwise, anything you send over the Zone you can kiss goodbye, because it's going to have a Tag missile on its ass that'll make it do pretty fireworks for the first and last time."

Garrison Duello's smile had broadened. "As my colleague just said, General," he confirmed, "if you want to fly anything at all over the Disputed Zone, you'll have to talk to us."

Later that morning, the General sped back to the Villa and called on the President. "It is my understanding," he told her, "that Parliament will meet tomorrow in emergency session to constitute an interim civilian pro-administration, pending the legal proceedings against you that will officially be opened today."

Vasilissa was contemptuous. "Aren't you forgetting that this state is a Convention signatory? WIASCO forces are over the border in Krastina, they're over the border in Ghimir, and their delegation is in this city right now. You are not going to get away with this."

"I'm afraid we already have," said the General, handing her the document he was holding. "Here is a copy of the accord reached between the Army and the Convention delegation. It guarantees the unimpeded course of the prosecution. They've left you to your fate. As for the Disputed Zone, responsibility for security is assumed by WIASCO, in collaboration with the Sardonikan Army and with the civilian pro-administration, once that has been formed."

Vasilissa snatched the papers from his hand and ran rapid eyes over them. The General stood by and waited for her answer.

At length, the President looked up. "I'll confer with my attorney," she said quietly. "You will hear from him."

Within an hour, General Leonidis walked into an office where Major Ravdos and a clutch of officers were milling around expectantly. "Gentlemen," the General announced, "I don't think it will be a surprise to anyone in this room when I say that our part in these events is coming to an end, and that the reopening of the airport will, as likely as not, mean that we and our families – I'm sorry – will be moving on." The hum of acknowledgement, the swallowed gall of the draught. "However, we have won a modest victory which, next to the pacification of our cities, satisfies me, at least, that it has not all been in vain." He paused, savouring the news for what it was worth. "The President has agreed to cooperate with the investigators."

It was not long after the General's announcement that he was approached by a senior officer who told him there was reason to fear an attempt by mercenaries to remove the President from the Villa. It would be wise, the officer counselled, to transfer the President secretly to Inner Command.

General Leonidis was vexed. The Inspector General would explode if he arrived at the Villa only to find that he had to make a further journey to interview the President. However, that explosion would break no bricks and claim no lives. And in the light of the warning that Monsignor Longhand had given him, the General had to consider that an external attempt to extract the President might have help from within. He authorized the transfer. The President, dressed anonymously in a jump-suit, was escorted from the Villa to a waiting helicopter, which rose up and soared west over the city.

Once it had flown beyond Kratistopolis Aiport, the helicopter flew an arc and circled back south-east, heading down towards the Disputed Zone. It was then that the President made radio contact with the WIASCO base in Krastina.

VASILISSA. This is the President of Sardoniki. I'm free and on my way to you.

WIASCO OPERATOR. Excuse me, Madam President, where are you?

VASILISSA. I'm coming to you by helicopter from the west. We're west of Kratistopolis, flying south-east over the Disputed Zone.

OPERATOR (*agitated*). Negative, negative, Madam President! The Invigilator's operational.

VASILISSA. The pilot's just transmitted the security code.

OPERATOR. Negative, negative! All previous codes are now non-recognized. Repeat: all previous codes now non-recognized. New codes not yet disclosed. Do not enter the Disputed Zone!

VASILISSA (*angry*). We're flying over the Zone now. The pilot's transmitted the code.

OPERATOR. When? How long ago was transmission?

VASILISSA. Four, five minutes ago.

OPERATOR. Oh shit.

VASILISSA (*shouting*). Stop! Where the hell are you going?

OPERATOR. What's happening? Madam President?

VASILISSA. He's bailing out! *Traitor!*

The satellite footage completes the account. The helicopter lurches appallingly as the parachute blooms beneath it. As the helpless machine drops, a Tag missile rushes close to it, dives to follow, and plunges into the helicopter as it wanders marooned in the air. A sheet of fire rises fiercely against the sky, then splits into acrid flames catching at the clouds.

# VIII.2. The Departing Passengers

Peter was in the kitchen when Leaina whirled in, exclaiming "Dead! Dead!" It was the feminine form of the adjective. As his hostess wheeled back into the living room, Peter hurried after her, to find Konon standing in surprise in front of the oracular screen.

"Who's dead?"

"The President. Blown up by her own killer satellite. The missile defence system that she sneaked in under cover of last Monday's rules."

Peter stood news-struck for a moment as his hosts continued to pay attention to the television. Then he turned and left the room again. The daunting presence felt six years ago, glimpsed two nights ago, gone. He had not spoken to her at her arrest. Should he have? But why, what would that have achieved? His own journey from hospital bed to roadblock via the Disputed Zone seemed now to have been an occult note of doom, a cryptic sound on the muffled trumpet of an archangel rising over the regions of the entombed and tombless dead. He made the sign of the Cross in the Latin manner.

"Peter!" Konon was calling him back into the room. "What time's your flight?"

"Why? The airport's not open again already, is it?"

"Think again! The General's done a deal. First effect: the airport's back in business."

Peter shook his head. If welcome and unwelcome things at once were hard to reconcile, how much more so when they were one and the same thing.

"Lady Alice is meant to be giving you her answer when you get home, isn't she?" Konon persisted.

"That's the idea."

"So what time is your flight?"

"It's supposed to be at four o'clock, but I imagine it's going to be chaos – "

"Come on!" cried Konon to Leaina. "We're going. This noble knight is not going to lose Fair Lady just because we didn't get him to the blasted airport on time." To Peter: "Go and pack your bag. No time to lose!"

Leaina started to protest, but Konon would have none of it. "Come on!" he cried. "Where's the car key?"

Peter finally gave in and laughed. "You're a mad bastard!"

Leaina pointed at her husband. "You see! Two of us are trying to tell you!"

"But if you insist – " said Peter, and quickly went to start packing.

Within half an hour they were driving back up the airport road. The traffic was nowhere near as heavy as Peter had feared. Probably, everyone else was keeping away, thinking that the airport would be too chaotic to approach. They parked, disembarked and moved quickly into the terminal, which exuded barely controlled disorder despite the manageable size of the clientèle. Peter checked in and pressed on, still accompanied by his hosts, towards security. They passed the information desk of a South American airline, where a familiar voice was raised in desperate incredulity.

"What do you mean there's no flight to Montevideo until tomorrow morning?"

They turned to see Khasra Khan, Mazil and Tishrab standing in front of the desk, luggage strewn about them.

"I'm sorry," said the girl behind the counter, "this evening's flight has been cancelled."

The Khan struck his forehead a resounding slap of pain and frustration. Mazil took up the dialogue. "There's no chance," he hazarded, "that the cancellation might be cancelled?"

"I really can't say."

Peter saw Tishrab turn despondently away from the company. He waved to the hapless youth and approached him, followed by Konon.

He knew he ought not to mock, but the situation called for some comment.

"Hi. How are you doing? You wouldn't like me to confirm any times, would you?"

Tishrab returned a contemptuous gesture, and began to turn away again. Peter saw the young man stiffen as Konstantinou's hand descended on his shoulder. The Khan and Mazil, too, became tense as they looked on. Surely neither Tishrab nor his companions really thought that Konon would break a man's neck in such a public place? On the other hand, after the experience of the last few days, one might be forgiven for no longer taking anything at all for granted.

"One word in your ear," Konon said with quiet urgency. "It's like what the bear says to the boy in the fable. If you follow *him* again – " (he looked straight at the Khan) " – and it gets you killed, then it really will be your fault." Raising his hand, he clapped Tishrab on the now-free shoulder and let him go. Then, with a respectful nod to Mazil, he rejoined his wife and Peter, and moved on.

Peter, his frame crushed by Konon and his hair ruffled by Leaina one last time, went through security and to his gate. Sit. Wait. Delay. Sit. Wait. Two hours behind schedule, no less, but no more. He boarded the sparsely populated plane and settled into his seat.

As the steel avian rose above the runway, Peter reflected that it had been but a week since he had flown in the opposite direction. Still, that had been a longer time in politics than anyone would have guessed. He looked out over the city where he had had his last, startling sight of Vasilissa Athemistou, shaken hands with the General, conferred with Ralph Longhand and kissed Maria Kalimithea as they said goodbye. Then he faced forward as the plane sped calmly on, still proceeding westward.

# VIII.3. He Who Sleeps

"Excuse me, Monsignor, there's someone here to see you. Miss Maria Kalimithea."

Ralph had the visitor sent into the parlour while he finished attending to his final piece of correspondence. He drew a question mark on a blank sheet of paper, folded it and put it in an envelope addressed to Father Grigorios. Writing *Longhand* on the back, he consigned it to the mail.

"What will you do now?" Maria asked him over tea.

"Take the first flight back to Rome," he said. "Now that the airport's open again, I shouldn't have too long to wait. There's no reason for me to stay since 'this Government' is no longer with us."

"Who do you think did it?"

"That's exactly what we're not meant to find out. But did you notice that no one seems to know who was flying the helicopter? Interesting, isn't it? You might want to point that out."

Maria put her tea down and scribbled a note in her pad.

"But that's not what you came to talk to me about, is it?" Ralph went on.

Maria shook her head, a little embarrassed. "'I haven't – I haven't said anything to my Editor about you."

"Just as well. I doubt he would have been impressed if he'd known you'd been passing information to Archbishop Theodoulos before writing it up."

"Then you knew I was the source?"

"It seemed likely enough. On Tuesday you came looking for me, because you knew who I was and what I was here for. Then, unexpectedly, Peter came your way. You kindly helped to rescue both of us, and then, when you learned that we knew each other, you thought there was a story behind it. So you did a little research. I did my best to keep my involvement in *that* incident out of the press, but I dare say you found the story on the site of some wretched local paper, am I right?"

She nodded, clearly pleased with herself.

"But Maria," he insisted, "you look after yourself in future. Keep away from old men behind desks who, like as not, are going to get you killed one of these days."

Maria smiled faintly. "Thanks for the warning. But there's a WIASCO press conference at the Institute this afternoon; my Editor wants me there."

"He's exploiting you! You deserve at least a month off. If I were you, I'd go home, shut the door and tell him where to stick his story."

"On the front page, Monsignor?"

"Precisely. On the front page. Now, Maria, if you'll excuse me, I have to go and pack."

*That incident*, he had called it: so he reflected once she had gone. It had begun as it had concluded, or, perhaps, as it was still continuing: under the sign of the martyr whose features had once looked out at him from a splendid icon, in a pub near Slightfield, of all places, two years previously. *Saint Dalmatios*, he had observed. *The patron of Sardoniki. Tenth century. Bishop and martyr. He who sleeps, let him wake up!*

These words had startled his hosts. He had explained. *Those are the saint's last words, according to the legend. A message for his countrymen in a time of trial.*

This had seemed strangely affecting to Alfred and Marion, but he had not wanted to pry. He took a different tack. *This is quite a piece, you know. One of the fourteenth-century masters, probably. If you don't mind my asking, where did you get it?*

SHE. *It belonged to our son. He'd been there, to Sardoniki, and brought it back with him. A gift from his friend, I think he said it was.*

HE. *If you have time tomorrow morning, we can take you to him. Then you'll see.*

The next day, as they drove along the rustic lanes, Ralph had wondered exactly where they were going. From the couple's sad tone, and from the way Marion had spoken of their son in the past tense, Ralph was more than half expecting to be taken to a cemetery. However, they had stopped in the car park of a nursing home. As they got out and made their way to the entrance, Ralph had noticed that Marion was carrying a bag with a hard, rectangular object inside it.

After they had walked on down a pastel corridor, Ralph had followed Alfred and Marion into a room off to the right, where a man was lying still in bed. His eyes were closed, and he was breathing normally, it seemed, but wrapped in an unnatural stillness. Ralph knew from the whole array of circumstances that the motionless figure was not merely asleep.

Then Marion had reached into her bag, drawing out the icon of Saint Dalmatios. Walking over to the dormant man, she had placed the icon on the bedside table. *There, that can keep him company.*

*That's our son*, her husband had explained. *Fifteen years in the Army. Four years ago he was sent to Sardoniki. They were clearing mines, and they were ambushed by guerrillas. Peter and his friend were the only ones who made it back. After he came home, he left the Army and got engaged.*

SHE. *Alice didn't want be an Army wife. So Peter left the Army and proposed to her again. But just after they got engaged –*

HE. *There was a leak in the house where he was staying. The water built up above the ceiling in the living room, and when Peter went in, the ceiling collapsed on his head. When he was found, he was lying flat out surrounded by water and rubble, with a third of the ceiling on the floor round about him.*

SHE. *And he's not moved or said a word since then. Sometimes I wonder if he can hear us but can't say anything back. But I don't know. I really don't know if we get through to him. He's just so – still.*

HE. *We were able to have him looked after here, thank God. At least here they look after him the way we want them to. No one's going to, well, take his tube out, you know. But if he's still like this when we're not here any more, well, you don't know, do you?*

At that point, Marion had shrieked. Ralph's first thought was that Alfred had upset her by bringing up the question of tube-feeding. But when he looked at Marion and her recumbent son, two things struck him in rapid succession. The first sight alone would have been startling enough. As for the second, he wondered if he could be sure that he had really seen it. He kept very quiet about it for a long time.

The first shock was that the man in the bed had opened his eyes. But that was not all. Ralph could have sworn that the saint in the icon had winked at him.

# Don't miss out!

Visit the website below and you can sign up to receive emails whenever Adam Scribentis publishes a new book. There's no charge and no obligation.

https://books2read.com/r/B-A-EKLCB-GGQCD

BOOKS 2 READ

Connecting independent readers to independent writers.

www.ingramcontent.com/pod-product-compliance
Ingram Content Group UK Ltd.
Pitfield, Milton Keynes, MK11 3LW, UK
UKHW040356100325
456003UK00001B/4

9 798224 437368